Tomb of Herihor

EDITH KUNZ

Edith Kunz

To my favorite Egyptophile, Donald R. Kunz

ACKNOWLEDGEMENTS

Donald Kunz, Jennifer Therieau, Mary DiRe Helmick, Dr. Kent Weeks, Dr. Richard Wilkinson, Riva Maria de Yares, Linda de Nazelle, Jessi Colter Jennings, Dr. Pablo Goldschmidt, Char & Sher, Professor Peter Lehman

They know what they did.

CHAPTER 1

Professor Surry Semaine did not have the reputation of a flirt, although he had a gregarious nature and natural charm that drew enthusiastic female students to his classes. The professor's expertise concerning erotic Egyptian hieroglyphs and rituals earned the unassuming archaeologist an eager following among both male and female admirers.

Surry's scholarly lectures about ancient Egypt were in popular demand, not only on the Arizona State University campus, but also by book clubs and historical conferences. His passion for Egypt's golden era filled Surry's long-limbed frame with a vitality that clearly confirmed that the man had found his bliss. Sharing his knowledge about the ancient Pharaonic era with those who were fascinated with past civilizations kept the professor's agenda actively engaged.

Fortunately, Valerie Semaine was a confident woman and could contend politely with the multitude of co-eds who found her husband attractive. As Valerie brushed her short chestnut hair in front of the mirror, the image that looked back at her appeared younger than her forty-two years. Often as she hurried across the university campus she was taken for one of the students rather than the wife of Professor Semaine, the school's respected authority on the Golden Age of Pharaohs.

Valerie was neither Hollywood beautiful nor New York chic, but she had the intellect and style sense that enhanced her trim figure with an individual presence. Attracting attention, however, was not a priority with Val. She was content to proudly watch her husband glow in his world of Egyptian folklore while she pursued her own undertakings.

Surry's focus in the world of ancient history made him appear as somewhat vague and quirky to many of his fellow professors. They admired his professionalism, but sometimes questioned whether their colleague was a dedicated genius, a calculating oddball, or a simple soul misplaced in modern times. His mind-drifts into past centuries often made his present day commitments and scheduling unpredictable. Minutes, hours, and days were trifles to him while his imagination loitered in exotic empires that existed five thousand years ago. It was Valerie's practicality that kept her esteemed mate on track within the present day requirements of teaching, writing and expedition schedules.

Like most serious archaeologists, Surry quietly daydreamed about discovering an undisturbed trove of precious artifacts or finding a lost or unexplored tomb. In reality even small finds such as tiny gold earrings were enough to thrill the professor during his summer expeditions along the Nile River. Although rarely verbalized, it was understood in the archaeological world that since that glorious day on November 4, 1922, when Howard Carter's team brushed away the sand on the first step down to the sealed doorway to Tutankhamen's tomb, the dream of every explorer was to find a major discovery of his own.

Sophisticated archaeologists are wary of revealing daydreams about a sensational discovery; however, Surry was fully aware that the vision hovered in his mind. There had been those candid moments between husband and wife when Surry blurted out boyish yearnings: "Herihor's mummy has to be out there somewhere, Val. Let's find it!"

Herihor, the rich and powerful Pharaoh who lived 2000 years before Christ, is documented in authentic scrolls of Egyptian hieroglyphs; however, the location of his actual tomb was still a mystery. Herihor, a name often whispered by adventurers around the globe, stayed current on the minds of explorers who dreamed of being the lucky one to solve the secret of this ancient ruler.

Surry Semaine often had time to daydream in the open spaces of the Arizona desert. He belonged to the ranks of conservationists who continued the effort to preserve what was left of the natural desert beyond the sprawling city of Phoenix. The sunny Southwest offered the professor and his wife an unpretentious lifestyle, as well as a vast terrain for scouting out Native American ruins during Surry's leisure time when free from his winter teaching schedule.

Even though university life churned with petty politics, the benefits for full professors made Surry's effort to comply with the teaching routine worthwhile. A full year's salary with two months off for research in Egypt served the simple needs of Surry and Valerie Semaine. Unless a person was independently wealthy, it was nearly impossible to prosper on the financial rewards of a full-time archaeologist. Surry's books, Mummification Rituals and Female Pharaohs, were successful enough to partially support the couple's annual summer research project in Egypt's Valley of the Kings.

Valerie gave up her teaching career for the necessity of

organizing her husband's manuscripts, lectures and travels. Surry's talents did not include handling details of living in present-day bureaucracy. They both longed for the day when they could afford to spend full time on writing, research and exploring in Egypt—a goal that appealed to Surry far more that lecturing in a classroom.

Valerie instinctively felt the devotion and loyalty of her husband, but she didn't delude herself about his priorities. She accepted this man for better or for worse, knowing deep down that his soul was centuries out of her reach. His addiction to past civilizations created within him an eerie detachment from the present world, leaving only a shadowy grip on personal relationships that he had been taught to hold dear. The professor's aloof aura was part of his character, to be politely accepted—or not—by those who knew him. He didn't dare confide to anyone how trivially he valued the mundane realities of his present life. He felt far more connected when he wandered back into the brilliant world of ancient Egypt where his restless soul rested comfortably. It was as if it had never been properly released from a past existence in pharaonic Egypt.

The telephone call from Charles Blumfield, which was about to change the conventional lives of the Semaines, was unexpected.

CHAPTER 2

"Charles Blumfield called today," Valerie announced when Surry returned from class. "Hard telling what that man wants now."

"He's probably ready to surface again after his last disaster," Surry said, as he pondered Blumfield's notoriously self-serving reputation. It was obvious that Charles was in need of a favor.

Charles Blumfield was considered persona non grata by Egypt's Supreme Antiquities Council. The wealthy adventurer had earned his disreputable status by bribing or bullying officials in his path while pursuing his interests along the Nile. He had foolishly employed these tactics three years earlier at Cairo's Egyptian Museum when his request to photograph the newly-uncovered Luxor Temple sculptures was refused. After bribing a museum curator, Blumfield proceeded to take photos of the newly acquired rare pieces. He then offered the photos to Archaeology Magazine before the Egyptian Antiquities Council released their own official press package. Such deceitful deeds may have gone unchallenged fifty years ago, but modern

Egyptians had learned hard lessons from their pillaged heritage and were zealously possessive of their remaining historical treasures and their marketing value.

The unauthorized premature publication of the new-found treasures made the Egyptian Archaeological Department look incompetent and foolish. They abruptly cancelled Blumfield's visitor's visa. In spite of the American businessman's generous donations to the country's archaeological preservation budget, he was no longer welcome in Egypt. While Egyptians may not live in a wealthy nation, as citizens they have a healthy supply of pride.

Surry Semaine smiled to himself when a sincere young voice answered in Blumfield's office. Charles usually kept a coterie of attractive assistants around him; he liked attractive surroundings and could afford his expensive tastes.

"Glad you called, Surry, it's been a while. I just read the current newsletter that you'll be speaking at the British Museum next April. Nice excursion for spring break, right?"

Surry recognized the insinuation that his lecture merely provided a free trip to London. Exactly the way Blumfield's mind operated. "Right, Charles, I'm on the program for the opening of the Rameses II exhibit. You plan to go?"

"I'll be there. It's hard to believe the Cairo Museum cut loose with so many prize artifacts. The show will be a stunner. While I'm in London, I want to discuss something that may interest you. We've known each other a long time, Semaine, and I like your style. I want to tell you about a big project. Lifetime big."

Such hype was common among archaeologists. They were an excitable bunch, always ready to envision the "next big find." Surry never tired of tomb tales, even if conveyed by a pompous fellow like Blumfield.

"We'll talk, Charlie. I arrive in London on April 14th and am on the agenda to speak the next morning. After my lecture and lunch with the museum staff, I'll have some free time."

"I can guarantee our chat will be worth your while, ole' boy. I'm staying at Brown's Hotel. Let's meet in the bar Thursday at five. You know the place, just off Knightsbridge?"

Surry knew exactly where the famous old hotel was located, even though his budget didn't allow the luxury of a five-star hotel. The dignified atmosphere of Brown's conveyed the spotless good taste that Charles Blumfield needed to mask his questionable reputation.

"Sounds fine, it'll be a nice walk from Eaton House where I'll be staying."

Blumfield's reply had a haughty tone. "Eaton House, never heard of it."

"Too bad, Charlie, it's a grand old mansion, but we insiders try to keep the place a secret. Hope you make it to my lecture."

Surry ended the conversation with a knowing smile. He knew Blumfield wouldn't trouble himself to show up for the lecture when he thought he knew far more about Egypt than a mere college professor.

CHAPTER 3

The Eaton House was a distinguished old townhouse that the proud proprietor, Ivan Iverson, had restored and opened as a boutique hotel. A friendly atmosphere permeated the roomy mansion and the modest bedrooms appealed to a savvy clientele. Iverson's head waiter, Mr. Blount, served a perfect English breakfast in the antique-filled dining room lined with faded Aubusson tapestries. The address of London's Eaton House was discreetly shared among academics as an opportunity to enjoy refined lodging on a scholar's budget. The creaky oak library filled with leather bound volumes provided a cozy setting for guests to unwind over an evening cognac at the "honor bar."

When Val did not travel with Surry, he rarely attended the London Theater or other evening offerings. He usually did not get around to securing tickets for cultural events unless it was arranged for him. No, when Surry was alone, his own company sufficed while he researched and dreamed of the next exploration in Egypt. The lure of ancient history never faded for Surry and he drifted back in time at every idle opportunity.

The lecture on Queen Nefertari, the favorite wife of Rameses II, which Surry delivered to the members of the British Museum, was augmented by a colorful video Surry had taken in the Queen's tomb. With his sincere zest for the topic, Surry was able to relay captivating details about the Egyptian artifacts displayed in the London Museum's exhibit. The audience got what they came for—a vivid, yet painless lesson about dynastic Egypt delivered with enthusiasm.

After lunch with a pleased museum staff, Surry took the big red bus to Eaton Place in time to stretch out on a feathery bed before the five o'clock meeting with Blumfield at Brown's Hotel. Surry stubbornly ignored jet lag, considering the subject overworked in too many boring conversations. Nevertheless, he was grateful for the opportunity to catch a quick nap.

Mr. Blount knocked on the door of Room 8 at four o'clock as requested. The persistent tapping awakened Surry from one of those deep daytime slumbers that fogs the mind. He strained to register the unfamiliar surroundings as he dropped his feet to the floor. He gazed at the floral chintz on the walls and the four-poster bed and began to make sense of his surroundings, but it took a vigorous shower to clear Surry's head and focus on the appointment ahead. Surry slipped into the jacket and trousers he had piled on the chair, knowing rumpled clothing would rarely be noticed among Londoners.

Semaine welcomed the bracing air of the damp English spring. He quickened his step to bypass the tempting bus stop and continued walking toward Hyde Park. He shot a respectful glance at Wellington's statue, and then headed toward Piccadilly Circus. The brisk walk was needed to sharpen his wits before facing Charles Blumfield. Odds were slight that the blow-hard would come up with anything worthwhile, but Surry could not resist the thought of a good tomb tale although one had to listen intently to sort out Blumfield's usual exaggerations.

The distinguished doorman with red coattails in front of Brown's Hotel conveyed respectability without appearing arrogant. Quiet dignity greeted visitors upon entering the staid lobby, where authentic antiques and thick Persian rugs left no question about the presence of privileged circumstances. A man felt compelled to wear a jacket and tie upon entering the place even though it was not a strict rule of the house, except for evening dinner. Oddly enough, the slightly disheveled Professor Semaine looked more like a "regular" in this stately hotel than the man in expensive Armani garb who greeted him. Blumfield's charcoal suit, mauve silk shirt and Hermes tie were so stylishly coordinated one expected a film crew to show up momentarily for a celebrity interview.

"Good to see you, Semaine. It's been a while. The gray hair makes you look like a seasoned academic. Bet you have to restrain the female students."

"You haven't changed, Charlie. Still women on the mind," chided Surry, sinking comfortably into one of the oversized chairs of the hotel's regal bar. "Val has a firm grip on my dance card. She manages to keep the co-eds at a safe distance." Surry suddenly wanted a beer. As for his having gray hair, the cad was mistaken. Lighter red, yes, gray...ridiculous!

The traditional tea hour was winding down and efficient waiters began removing white linens from the mahogany tables, replacing the trays of pastries with macadamia nuts and freshly baked chips. Surry's Guinness came in a frosted mug along with Blumfield's gin martini.

"What's on your mind, Charlie?" inquired Surry, sinking back in the leather armchair with the frosted brew.

"There's a lot on my mind, Professor. I've thought a long time about a partner in this deal and I'm convinced you're the one. Nobody else qualifies."

"Before I'm flattered, just what did I qualify for? You are aware that I'm not keen on shady deals."

Granted, Surry had been acquainted with this man for twenty years, but mostly in the gossipy gatherings at archaeological conferences. Both men had excavated in the Valley of the Kings, but were never on the same team. Blumfield's expeditions operated on a more extravagant budget than Surry's university-sponsored digs. The wealthy entrepreneur and his crew hung out in the deluxe Winter Palace Hotel while Surry's team lodged in one of Luxor's nondescript small hotels. It never entered the professor's mind to collaborate with a person like Charles, even though the financial benefits were enviable. They were different sorts, exploring the Sahara Desert for entirely different motives. Surry craved the stimulation of discovery, while Charles obviously longed for attention and fame.

"What I'm about to tell you is a legit deal, Surry. Can I trust you?"

"Probably more than most of your other cronies," Surry injected with a snicker.

"Well, professor, how about a hot lead on Herihor?"

Trying to conceal the rush of blood that surged within him, Surry Semaine drained the beer, stalling for words. He often dreamed of Herihor's tomb, but why must he hear that revered pharaoh's name from a bloke like Blumfield?

"Intriguing thought, Charlie, what do you have? Experts smarter than you have been hunting Herihor for centuries.

What makes you so lucky?"

"I make my own luck, pal, by spending big bucks doing research with the right folks. Tomb raiders know more about the Valley of the Kings than your fancy school books and, for the right price, information is available. Even skeptics like you might be impressed with this." Blumfield's hand cautiously withdrew a small blue velvet bag from an inside pocket. "And no preaching ethics, Semaine. This bauble rightfully belongs to me. I paid for it."

Surry nodded absently, his eyes fixed on the object Charles pulled from the pouch. The people occupying the comfortable old chairs in the hotel lounge had changed from the afternoon teatime crowd to affluent types focused on politics and economics. The two American explorers were ignored by nearby guests, allowing Charles to hold the curious item unnoticed.

Carefully Blumfield held the cylinder-shaped object of yellow metal in the palm of his hand. The markings of a finely-shaped masculine toe were apparent in the delicately-crafted gold piece. Surry immediately recognized the artifact as a "toe stall," which ancient Egyptians used to protect the toes of princely corpses before a mummy was wrapped in linen bandages.

Surry resisted the urge to reach out for the article, determined to control his composure. "It's an impressive item. The only other one I've seen of that quality was Tutankhamen's. How sure are you this thing is authentic?"

"Oh, it's real alright. I've done my homework. It is known that pharaohs had duplicates made of accessories, such as these toe guards for their eternal life in the underworld. My contacts in Egypt evidently came across this prize during one of their scavenger forays. I bought the set of ten, all with Herihor's marking. I have something else, too."

To an enthusiast like Surry, the mark on a gold artifact like the one Blumfield was holding was enough to make his trip across the ocean worthwhile. If real, it was a priceless museum piece, and here it was, casually flaunted before his eyes. With any of his associates other than the rogue seated across from him, Surry would have been exuberant, but with Blumfield he hesitated to show his true excitement.

"It's a good one," breathed Semaine, tentatively reaching toward the glowing object. "May I examine it?"

"I don't see any museum guards around, do you? Turn it over. The cartouche is on the back. Looks like Herihor's symbol to me."

Surry felt a rush of warmth when the gold toe stall touched his hand. What he held was a precious item, perhaps crafted by an artist who existed thirty-five hundred years ago. If this were the real thing, it rightfully belonged in a museum, properly preserved and shared with scholars.

"You have my attention, Charles. Where do I fit in? If you have a lead on Herihor and the funds to go after him, why tell me about it? Just to watch me squirm?"

"I'm not into giving men a thrill, Semaine. I prefer women, although I must say your expression amuses me. No, Professor, you have a valuable asset to add to the project—your reputation. I guess you heard that I had a run-in with the Department of Antiquities and they cancelled my visitor's visa. I need a partner with a valid research permit from an educational institution, someone who already has a planned project in line for this summer. This could merely be a clandestine sideline activity for you."

Blumfield had a point; Surry gave him credit for that much. At least the rich boy could recognize ethics in someone else, even though his own were questionable.

There weren't many blemishes in Surry's past and, except for a few youthful college pranks, his credentials were impeccable.

Personal integrity was important to Surry. He didn't stray far off course often without paying the price of remorse. A traditional Midwestern upbringing imbued Surry with a solid sense of morality.

Surry avoided associating with disreputable types like Charles Blumfield, as he knew such relationships seldom end well. So why couldn't the professor pull himself away from the unsavory fellow now facing him?

There are peepholes of temptation, even in the most virtuous souls, and the gold toe stall had managed to pierce that gap in Surry's principles. Holding an object that was made for a pharaoh's foot three thousand years ago fueled Surry's fantasy for ancient treasures and jumbled his judgment.

The reign of the Pharaoh Herihor following Rameses XI's death in 1070 B.C. was a favorite topic among archaeologists. Folklore, legends and historical documentation indicated that Herihor had confiscated sacred treasures from many majestic temples and royal tombs to "protect" them in his closely-guarded funerary chamber, perpetuating the long-held assumption that huge riches waited in his unfound tomb.

Herihor reigned during an era when grave robberies were rampant and were of major concern to priests and nobles. Herihor's order to transfer treasures from other sacred venues for "safe keeping" had to be accepted as a king's mandate. Without doubt the wealthy Pharaoh's final resting place, piled high with confiscated riches, had been hidden with great care. Today's historians consider Herihor to be a tomb robber of sorts himself, and locating his vast collection of precious goods could prove to be one of Egypt's greatest discoveries. Locating the lost tomb of this 20th-dynasty ruler had long been a fantasy of Egyptologists worldwide, all fully aware that artifacts from multiple reigns accumulated by Herihor in one stockpile would have enormous value as well as great historical significance.

"What evidence do you have besides the toe stall? And what makes you trust the word of tomb robbers, Charlie?"

"Don't worry about that, I know how to deal with desert rats. They'll spill anything if the price is right. Forget religion, history or honor; money motivates them, and they know I've got plenty. Actually, it's not those scoundrels I'm concerned about, Semaine, it's the crafty Egyptian officials who'll be the first to cause me trouble."

"So, what's your plan? People involved in schemes behind the backs of Egyptian officials can end up in an Arab prison. Consequences could be even worse when you're dealing with the black market crowd."

"You know damn well, Semaine, there's always a risk involved with excavating the tombs. This deal is no riskier than other high-stake gambles. All must be planned perfectly. There's too much to lose by being careless. That's why I want reputable people like you on the team. This find would make international headlines."

Charles Blumfield was a master with words and he used the right ones to bait Surry Semaine. Herihor, lost tomb, burial treasures…like wiggling worms in front of a fish. The professor struggled to suppress a growing exhilaration while his better judgment was overpowered by boyish dreams of discovery. The undeniable passion in Surry's gaze did not escape Blumfield's scrutiny; he could see that his prize catch was hooked. Charles proceeded to troll Surry in with bits and pieces of an offer.

Without detailing the supposed location of the pharaoh's tomb, Blumfield outlined his scheme to hunt down the lost king's burial treasures. Such a discovery could fill a mystifying link in the pharaonic lineage and would be sensational news for Egyptologists all over the world. For the red-headed professor from Arizona State University, participating in such a find would be a dream come true.

Although outwardly the two men engrossed in conversation in the hotel lounge appeared to be in perfect accord, their goals registered differently in each of their minds. Fame, glory and power flashed on Blumfield's mental screen, while Surry's skin prickled with the thought of finding wondrous artifacts in a royal tomb.

The imagination of the jittery professor soared. It made little difference whether he was hearing truth or hype; the captivating picture that Blumfield laid before him was enough to grip his attention. Ideally, Surry would have preferred this story from a more reputable source, but history-making opportunities do not always arrive in perfect packages.

Pompously, Blumfield boasted of possessing a map leading to Herihor's lost tomb. Charles stated that after dealing in tomb relics with the infamous Mostfa clan for twenty years, they had presented him with a startling proposal. Knowing that Blumfield paid big money for quality merchandise, the thieves felt secure enough to offer the prize of a lifetime—a map to the lost tomb of Herihor.

The illicit trade of stolen burial goods was everyday business in the Sahara Desert. For centuries, families connected with robbing burial sites continued to hand down corrupt skills from generation to generation. Lately, the notorious Mostfa family was shaken by a crackdown from the new Director of Supreme Antiquities Council, who was a devoted historian intent on stricter rules to preserve Egypt's heritage. Illegal dealers were forced to develop a new strategy of selling information rather than actual goods, leaving foreigners to take the risk of looting while the scoundrels were miles away with cash safely in their pockets.

Charles had not hesitated when he was invited to meet Ali Mostfa in Athens earlier in the year to examine exceptional objects. After careful examination of the gold toe shield and the sketchy map of Herihor's tomb, Charles paid dearly for the items. Never mind that he lacked a valid permit to explore in Egypt's desert. In fact, Blumfield didn't even have the right to enter the country, but such barriers did not deter a man like Charles from going after what he wanted.

Blumfield's devious mind welcomed challenges with relish. He came up with the brilliant idea to involve the respected Professor Surry Semaine. The clean-cut academic was a recognized authority on Ancient Egypt with valid credentials, an author of successful publications, as well as having several documented digs in the Valley of the Kings to his credit.

Surry's quiet confidence made him popular among his associates, shielding him from the usual petty jealousies that plagued most treasure-seekers. His access to Arizona State University's research funds was of importance to Egyptian authorities who were forever on the lookout for foreign money to help continue explorations into Egypt's glorious past.

In spite of his glaring character flaws, Blumfield was not a fool. He had studied the options carefully and Surry fulfilled the conditions perfectly. A clever choice; in fact, maybe too good.

CHAPTER 4

Unlike Blumfield, the Professor was not accustomed to juggling rules. Through serious dedication, Surry was able to generate enough demand for his talents without the need to overstep regulations.

Being the absentminded savant that he was, Surry considered laws a convenient way of reminding him when to pay taxes, renew a passport, stop at a red light, stay off the grass, purchase a ticket before entering and other such rules of a civilized existence. Laws took care of daily details that Valerie was too busy to organize for her husband. Surry's only real interest in the legal system and politics was finding the least complicated routes to desirable sites of exploration.

Aided by the scholarly genes scattered in his DNA, Surry had evolved into a practical individual brought up by a Midwestern family of teachers who valued human decency. Rosemary and Arthur Semaine were proud of their boy. In Cedar Rapids, Iowa, it was important to have well-behaved kids. A family's bad deeds got around in a small community and foul public habits tainted the whole clan.

The protective lifestyle in the Midwest was just right for a loner like Surry. At school he was accepted in the gang as the "quiet and studious guy." He graduated valedictorian of Cedar Rapids High, although his honors did not include trophies in sports or dating. There were a few chums he casually played tennis with, but Surry didn't go out of his way to fill his free time with socializing or sports. The happiest times of Surry's youth were spent in the attic, building model fortresses and directing toy armies into battle or merely drifting off with a book into the world of knights, kings and pharaohs.

When the sensational discovery in 1987 of the long lost tomb of Sons of Rameses II hit world headlines, Surry was in his junior year at the University of Iowa. The dramatic news of "Kings Valley #5" sparked ambitions of adventure in the young daydreamer's mind and he collected every shred of information he could find on the excavation process taking place in the Valley of the Kings.

Surry pointed his studies toward a degree in Middle Eastern Studies, a choice which concerned Rosemary and Arthur Semaine. It was worrisome how their boy would support himself with such qualifications; however, they hesitated to derail the son who had rarely caused them alarm until this expensive red flag in his educational intentions.

The flame of Surry's Egyptian interests flared up when he became immersed in the celebrated Ancient History sector of the University Library. It was one of those ideal educational connections when a gifted student is sparked by the right resources suited to his passion. Surry's determination and perseverance paid off and he received a prized Egyptology Study Scholarship at the end of his sophomore year. It allowed the motivated student to join the undergraduate team of a Harvard archaeological professor for summer studies in Luxor, Egypt. That summer was the beginning of a long and dusty career.

The young explorer's mind was sufficiently nourished by ancient pot shards and bone fragments allowing him to remain content to sift sand for years before noticing the needs of manhood. Valerie Benson, a pretty team member from the University of Washington, made discoveries of her own while sifting sand beside Surry. The desires of the young lady began to heat up well before Surry took notice of her attempts to lure him toward romance.

One afternoon he experienced an unfamiliar sensation when he and Val were surveying the dimly lit tomb of Yuya and Tjuyu. The sensuously carved breasts of an Egyptian goddess suddenly captured the young archaeologist's attention and for the first time since meeting Valerie he was aware of the mounds of flesh rising and falling under her thin cotton blouse. He noted with curiosity his own male mound also rising near his front pocket.

Instinctively the young man reached for Valerie's extended hand as she guided him further down the darkened passageway toward the royal couple's burial chamber. From the moment of that first clumsy kiss in Yuya's tomb, Valerie and Surry became a united team, bonded by their archaeological discoveries as well as the discoveries of their own bodies. Surry was in charge of the mental forays, while Valerie happily led the more carnal explorations. Their first months as a couple were filled with exhilarating bursts of passionate learning in the steamy Sahara.

With her sights set on the studious university student from the Midwest, Valerie transferred to the University of Iowa to complete her degree in anthropology as well as to secure her grip on Surry Semaine. She was perceptive enough to accept Surry's obsession with ancient Egypt and knowledgeable enough to contribute to his pensive conversations about the Pharaohs. Val cleverly wrapped herself around Surry's mind and body until the habit became an accepted part of his life.

Valerie gently led her precious savant toward the comforts and conveniences of marriage before such thoughts fully formed in the young man's mind. As a team, they were ready to research the past and future together. Surry's parents were fond of Valerie and her caring and capable ways which relieved them from the concern of their pensive son's vague lifestyle.

The partnership worked. Surry and Valerie managed well in their muddled world of simple possessions and joyful expeditions. Supported by scholarly grants, published papers and academic employment, the couple enjoyed a contented existence of teaching and research that fulfilled their basic needs and intellectual objectives. What was ahead for them was beyond their simple desires.

CHAPTER 5

It took a devious rogue named Charles Blumfield to come up with a mysterious tomb map that would tempt Professor Semaine to consider deeds of deceit. Blumfield's primary desire was to discover a lost Pharaoh's tomb and wallow in world acclaim, while probing ancient mummies was what stirred Surry's dreams of discovery.

In spite of the shadowy light in Brown's Hotel Bar, Charles was able to observe the engrossed trance the gold toe seemed to cast over the contemplative professor.

"Think it over, Semaine," Charles injected into the stillness of Surry's reverie. "But we'll have to act on this before someone else gets wind of this."

"Yes…yes…right," Surry murmured. "Rumors can leak out…I've gotta sleep on it. I'll call you tomorrow before I leave for the airport."

The two men walked through the regal lobby of the hotel toward the doorman at the entrance. Surry and Charles made an unlikely pair. Their clothing, haircuts and shoe shines were not from the same side of town.

"So long, Semaine. I'm heading for Asprey's for a few

take-home gifts," Blumfield proclaimed proudly, giving Surry an "ole boy" handshake. "Think hard, my friend, opportunities like this are rare. I'll cut loose with details when you say the word."

"I'll let you know." Surry's voice trailed off as he turned mechanically toward Piccadilly Circle. While his instincts continued to warn him to stay clear of Charles Blumfield, the thought of finding Herihor outweighed his sense of caution.

The polished oak door of Eaton House suddenly loomed before him as if he had been magically transported across town by an unknown force. He didn't recall passing Wellington's statue, the trees in Hyde Park, the noise in Sloane Square or for that matter any of the traffic lights that had somehow guided him safely along his way. Other matters occupied his mind, more absorbing than the swift London traffic that he had managed to avoid on his way back to Eaton Place.

Surry's ingrained ethics, rooted by his respectable upbringing, blocked the growing desire to telephone Charles Blumfield immediately, to seal the partnership and find out just how much the scoundrel really knew about Herihor. Surry ignored the urge to pick up the phone as soon as he entered his small room; it was not his habit to act impulsively and his mind was worn-out.

Blumfield had proposed a scheme which seemed to circumvent the Egyptian authorities and overlook government regulations. Much of the advice that Surry preached in his classrooms would be compromised by any association with such a furtive plan. The idea was not much better than a pirate venture, similar to the ruthless tactics of the irresponsible nineteenth century tomb raiders.

Alone in his hotel, grim images of Giovanni Belzoni's

careless excavations in the early 1800's began to weigh heavily on Surry's mind as he sank into the feather comforter, lifting his stocking feet to rest on the foot board of the antique bed.

A dark picture emerged as Surry drifted off to sleep. Blumfield would be basking safely in the California sunshine if Egyptian officials became suspicious about Surry's unauthorized dig. The onus of guilt would rest entirely on Professor Semaine and his reputation as a trusted educator would be permanently tarnished, resulting in banishment from the Nile Valley. To risk a career of dedicated research on such an elusive endeavor might be intriguing to contemplate, but to gamble one's name on mere chance was recklessness unaccustomed to Surry.

It was dawn when Surry finally awakened with gnawing hunger pangs. He had slept the night in his rumbled clothes, completely missing the previous evening's dinner hour. Two cups of black coffee were Surry's usual morning requirement; however, this did not feel like a routine day. Herihor had filled his dreams during the night and continued to invade Surry's waking thoughts. The desire for breakfast was not nearly as compelling as his obsession to talk with Blumfield.

Surry Semaine was a man who had turned down smoking pot with his peers, who felt guilty if he cheated on taxes, who stayed faithful to his wife, who crossed the street at crosswalks…a man who was comfortable with rules. However, Charles Blumfield had found the path to Surry's weak spot and the professor was ready to try a moral detour. A man who had never before been tempted by recreational drugs was now hallucinating on a thrill offered by a conniving pusher.

Surry dialed Blumfield's hotel room. "I'm interested,

Charles. I'll plan to fly to San Francisco next week and we can talk about details then."

CHAPTER 6

Valerie Semaine did not have a penchant for illicit acts. On the other hand, she didn't turn away in disgust when snippets of sin were waved in front of her. Dealings that appeared to Surry as unquestionably black might look merely gray to Val. Perhaps her Italian ancestors had donated a gene that tolerated varying degrees of roguery. Valerie and Surry were in accord that Blumfield was beyond the limits of a harmless rascal. It was questionable how far the man would go to achieve his desires; nevertheless, Charles gave the impression that he was capable of harming people without much pain to his conscience.

"Very bizarre," murmured Valerie after hearing Surry's London report as they drank their morning coffee in Arizona, "but then tomb adventures always seem to have an undeniable attraction even when surrounded by intrigue."

"Well, if true, this one has huge possibilities." Surry's voice trailed off as he gazed at the sunrise through the large kitchen window. "The desert looks good to me after foggy London. You look good to me, too. I'm going to need your help dealing with this guy."

Valerie put her coffee down and stood behind Surry

pressing her body against his warm shoulders. "Let's think carefully about this. You know that you are my hero whether you discover a pharaoh's tomb or not."

"You're right, Val, Egypt doesn't seem quite so important when I'm home with you in Arizona. Must confess though, locating Herihor's tomb is a big temptation. It sounds risky, but hard to pass up. Do you think we could put together a legitimate project with a partner like Blumfield?"

"It's not easy to stay ethical when dealing with that fellow. He's slippery," Val answered with a slight shudder.

"Well, the plus side is that he's not allowed into Egypt and he won't be there to harass us if we go ahead with the plan. Guess that's why he needs me for the grunt work. We're going to Egypt this summer anyway. Shall I go to San Francisco, Val, and hear what the rogue has to say? Herihor's tomb is out there somewhere and I'll be damned if I want to wait around for someone else to find it."

CHAPTER 7

The flight from Phoenix to Cairo, with a plane change in London, lasted a wearisome fifteen hours, relieved somewhat by upgrade coupons, an unfamiliar luxury for the frugal teachers. This trip didn't feel like the other times they had traveled to the Sahara Desert loaded with books, cameras, survey equipment and mosquito repellent. Something extra had been added: the small notebook with rough sketches of Luxor's West Valley.

The hand-drawn map with coded initials was stashed securely in Surry's leather belt pack. Merely knowing it was there sent his imagination spinning. Envisioning Herihor's rich funerary stockpile, Surry fell into a hazy trance lulled by the steady whine of jet engines.

Driving away from the small Luxor airfield in a battered station wagon can plunge a visitor into a time gap far more dramatically than a simple clock adjustment. Biblical traditions still governed the pace and tone of Luxor's easygoing inhabitants. Leathery-skinned men in robes and sandals led loaded donkeys along the narrow thoroughfares, undaunted by passing cars and tourist buses. Along the road, sturdy palm trees lined the irrigation ditches, where oxen monotonously pulled the ropes that lifted water buckets from the ancient canals for the young boys who distributed water to the nearby rows of cotton.

The worn-out taxi bumped along, but the exhilaration of being back in Luxor diminished Val and Surry's discomfort from the hot, dusty air and pungent smoke from the driver's cigarette. When the vehicle stopped in front of the Nefertari Hotel, the grinning cabbie took Surry's money without any effort to either return change or help unload the couple's baggage.

The Semaines were familiar with the modest Nefertari Hotel from past visits, and did not waste time waiting for a non-existent doorman. It was late afternoon when they carried their baggage into the deserted reception area. Only a few circling flies interrupted the silence of the dim room before Valerie tapped the chrome bell on the counter near the entrance. Surry glanced at his wife with a knowing half-smile.

The obvious nonchalance that greeted them in the drab lobby was not a surprise. The family-owned lodging made up for its inconveniences by offering low weekly rates, adequate meals and proximity to the local ferry that crossed the Nile to the Valley of the Kings. The rooms were reasonably clean and equipped with a private bathroom, an electric fan and a telephone which worked most of the time. Morning coffee and toast were included in the room rate, and acceptable sheets and towels were changed twice a week.

"Welcome, welcome, Doctor Semaine," greeted Amed, emerging from the dangling beads shielding his dwelling behind the desk. "Welcome to Luxor. We know you are coming today. We are pleased you are with us again. The room is ready," Amed said proudly in English with minimal regard toward Valerie. In Amed's culture, men took precedence.

The third-floor room that the Semaines preferred was on the corner overlooking the Nile, just high enough to muffle the noisy chatter of the carriage drivers' hangout below and not too high to manage the stairs when the lone elevator malfunctioned.

"Home sweet home for the next two months," whispered Val, reclining on the firm mattress with two thin pillows. She scanned the drab room, eyeing the simple armoire and faded curtains. "Can't you just see Blumfield staying here?"

"Not a chance...nothing less than a Nile view at the Winter Palace for that guy," scoffed Surry, as he methodically arranged his underwear in the shallow drawer of the bureau. "Charlie has never fit in with the rest of the archeologists. He had his own bankroll and went his own way."

Valerie's eyelids were heavy, "Guess we shouldn't badmouth the man now that we've decided to team up with him. I hope it's not a big mistake...he's tricky."

"Too late to worry now, my dear. What do you say we eat our apples and get some sleep? I'm too tired to go out for dinner."

"I'm for sleep, too. Let's get an early start in the morning and see what's waiting for us across the Nile."

Yes. There was plenty waiting for Surry and Valerie in the Cemetery of the Pharaohs.

CHAPTER 8

For centuries Luxor had been a popular destination for adventurous tourists, but not a town for those who depended upon the luxuries of the Western World. Even the wealthy travelers staying at one of the few first-class hotels cannot always avoid mosquitoes, intestinal ailments, rancid smells from the alleys, and the risk of terrorism. For over a hundred years, affluent English visitors have checked into the legendary Winter Palace Hotel for the warm spring season. Sun-starved Londoners can bask by the hotel's shaded swimming pool and eat in the gourmet restaurants while they ignore the hardships of local Egyptians beyond the high walls of the exclusive resort. Privileged guests stay comfortably separated from the working population, except for the neatly uniformed native service staff.

When rich foreigners wish to view the Valley of the Kings, they cross the Nile in private yachts and have their touring cars sent over on the ferry. Wealthy tourists can daydream in the backseat of air-conditioned cars while taking in the highlights of ancient monuments before returning to the comforts of the palatial hotel on the East Bank. Not many archaeologists or university professors can afford such deluxe amenities, except for playboys like Charles Blumfield, who pursued the mysteries of the Sahara Desert as an amusement and an excuse for his usefulness.

Egypt's stifling summers catered to bargain hunters, tour groups, courageous student travelers and teachers with meager budgets. Surry Semaine didn't consider his austere circumstances a hindrance to the joy he derived from digging among the local ruins. Even during the dangerously hot afternoons, Surry took such pleasure in his project that he had to be reminded to take shelter from the debilitating sun. Valerie was there to rub sunscreen on Surry's fair skin, to place a brimmed hat over his faded red hair, and to encourage him to drink plenty of water. When Surry rummaged around the desert rocks, he did not pay attention to the dangers of the real world.

On their first full day in Luxor, the Semaines picked up the customary permits and papers which they had arranged months before leaving America. They paid dutiful visits to the bureau chief of the Supreme Antiquities Council and the Inspector General of Luxor Monuments and presented both with modest gifts, which were discreetly tucked away in office drawers. After an outline of the Arizona team's agenda was officially filed and fees paid, current identification passes for members of the team were issued.

The mission report for the university project listed the primary task as "verification of survey records and publication of new findings relating to the crumbling tomb of Amenhotep III." What was left of the pillaged mummy of the great 18th-dynasty Pharaoh Amenhotep had been removed by priests during an early era of rampant tomb robberies. High priests at that time carried out several royal mummies and secretly hid them to avoid further destruction by bandits. After extensive damage caused by ancient tomb robbers and careless explorers, the sacred site of Amenhotep III was barely recognizable as the once-decorated resting place of a powerful king.

Over the centuries, bands of thieves had pillaged the priceless burial goods, leaving behind only remnants of the granite sarcophagus, which was reportedly removed by priests for other noble burials. It was Howard Carter who rediscovered the West Valley of Amenhotep III tomb in 1905, but found little to interest him in the shambles of the robbed crypt. He cleared some of the rubble in the burial chamber and then proceeded to use the front hallway of Amenhotep's tomb as a storage room for excavating equipment while he probed nearby sites.

This neglected cavern of Pharaoh Amenhotep still had enough hidden nooks and crannies to pique the interest of Surry and Valerie Semaine. Scrutiny of the faint hieroglyphs, barely visible in the corroded tunnels, continued to attract the dedicated couple from Arizona. The map that Surry kept securely hidden in his money belt was far more fascinating to him than what was within Amenhotep's final resting place.

Professor Semaine's summer working schedule began with a four o'clock wake-up call. One could never be certain that the laid-back desk clerk would remember an early morning request, but Valerie answered the phone at 4:05 a.m. and leisurely stretched. Surry's eyes, however, opened immediately. He needed no coaxing to get up when Egyptian tombs awaited him. He unlatched the shutters and surveyed the softly lit street below which was filling with the muffled sounds of horses being hitched to carriages. A faint golden glow outlined the mountain range in the East, hinting at waves of heat on their way to the Nile Valley.

After a cup of instant coffee made with lukewarm tap water, Valerie began to function with a quicker step. She slid in and out of Surry's shower for a fast rinse while her husband continued his fastidious scrubbing. Dressing for work in the Sahara Desert was a routine matter. Both wore simple khaki pants, long-sleeved shirts and multi-pocketed vests where money, ID papers, film, Pepto-Bismol, notes and pencils could be kept securely. They never failed to remember a liter of bottled water, knowing that an hour or two without water in the desert sun could render one ineffective long before the warning of thirst.

The Nefertari Hotel's small dining room was deserted at five in the morning, not that the austere room was able to draw a crowd at any time of day or night. The skinny Arab waiter arrived as soon as the Semaines sat down. There was no need for a menu because breakfast was always the same: strong black coffee, hard-boiled eggs, coarse flat bread and fresh oranges. The eager pair did not linger over the plain food, taking their oranges to eat during the short ferry ride across the river.

The path to the public ferry landing was already bustling with chattering merchants pushing carts packed with live chickens, stacks of round brown bread, eggs, melons, and bolts of cotton that the West Bank villagers waited for each morning. Rows of wooden benches with tarps overhead awaited the passengers aboard the open-air ferry. The older Arab women clustered together, talking amongst themselves, forming a maze of black flowing gowns, while the men gathered in a circle of fluttering blue *jelabiyas* to share cigarettes and local news.

The native merchants who rode the ferry each morning were a smiling bunch, enjoying the peaceful river crossing before the arduous routine of hawking their wares on the other side. Cool morning breezes made the twenty-minute crossing one of the most pleasant experiences of a worker's day.

As the only Americans aboard the "people's ferry," Val and Surry were closely observed with stares of benevolent curiosity. The tattered shoeshine boy headed directly to the foreigners with his homemade wooden box, diluted shoe polish and donkey tail brush. The persistent lad labored over Surry's boots, joyfully charging him double the local price, which Surry gladly paid just to see the thin boy's toothy smile when he handed over two American dollar bills.

After docking, Valerie and Surry followed the swarming crowd down the wobbly metal plank and immediately caught sight of Mohammed's waving arms motioning them toward his car. Egyptian taxi drivers were surprisingly reliable, especially when tourists were in short supply and customers were scarce. Mohammed, who had driven for the professor in years past, seemed genuinely happy to see him. He showed obvious pride among the other waiting drivers to be recognized by his American customers.

Valerie and Surry were equally grateful to spot the familiar face in the blur of turbaned vendors shouting the merits of wares and services. They gripped Mohammed's extended hand and crawled into the back seat of the faded blue Peugeot, sliding across the camelhair blanket which protected passengers from the sunbaked plastic seat. As soon as the engine turned over, the driver proudly switched on the battery operated fan which taped to the dashboard. Mohammed's agile ability to weave in and out of donkey carts and potholes compensated for the vehicle's soiled condition.

It was particularly useful for foreigners to be

accompanied by a respected local citizen known to the checkpoint guards, as well as a driver who could navigate the unmarked roads. Mohammed was more cautious than other drivers who made a game of darting in and out of the tour buses that lined the narrow asphalt route to the Valley of the Kings. Complications of a vehicle accident in Egypt terrified Westerners, considering the scary stories told of local first-aid practices and primitive medical facilities. The possibility of being held responsible for a dead donkey or injured native was not an uncommon occurrence when tourists were involved in traffic accidents, promoting lucrative scams among cab operators.

At the last bend leading to the entrance of the Royal Cemetery, the taxi detoured to the historic Howard Carter House which now served as a residence for Egyptian officials. It was a strict requirement for every foreign excavation team to employ a government supervisor to observe proceedings that went on at historic sites.

Archaeological supervision had become more controlled by Egypt's current Minister of Culture. Inspectors were instructed to stop the flow of precious artifacts carried away illegally. Too many of the country's relics had been stolen, abused and commercialized during past centuries and Egyptian officials were clamping down on the disappearance of prized treasures.

Inspector Rachid emerged from the white stucco villa that had previously housed the famed Howard Carter when he discovered King Tut's tomb. The bronzed-skin Egyptian walked swiftly through the manicured vegetable garden toward the approaching Peugeot, recognizing the Semaines from the year before. Rachid was a former security guard and displayed a sense of superiority in his new uniform of a full-fledged inspector. He embraced the professor warmly while accepting the laser flashlight that Surry slipped discreetly into the inspector's hand. Rachid was not ready to jeopardize his important new job by taking monetary gifts, but the sleek lantern was too appealing to refuse.

The official wore neat tan trousers, a cotton shirt with black shoulder boards, sturdy desert boots and the customary white gauze turban. He confidently took his place of authority next to the cab driver, motioning Mohammed to continue driving toward the royal necropolis.

The curving two-lane road through the rocky cliffs to the King's Cemetery never failed to make Surry's flesh quiver. Awareness of other passengers in the car became blurred while Surry's thoughts drifted to visions of the many funeral processions that had trudged through the same canyon thousands of years ago. Surry feel superbly alive.

Valerie nudged Surry from his reverie when the car stopped at a blockade next to a whitewashed guard house. Mohammed waited in the cab as the three passengers paid a mandatory visit in the controller's windowless mud-brick office. Surry and Valerie accepted the glass of hot mint tea as they patiently waited for their host to give the standard welcome speech. It was imperative for foreign archaeologists to stay on good terms with local bureaucrats, as permits for excavation in Egypt were not based purely on academic qualifications. To be trusted by native officials was equally important. The chief's slight grin acknowledged the small portable fan that Surry left on his desk.

The dusty vehicle proceeded cautiously through the lifted barrier toward the famous tombs of Tutankhamen, Rameses II and Rameses III. Half way up the hill, the driver was instructed to turn right onto a gravel road that forked off from the paved route. The university's work site was located west of the more famous royal site, in a desolate canyon called the West Valley that rarely enticed travelers to visit the lesser-known tombs that existed there.

Although Surry and Val had taken the same bumpy road many times, they were not immune to the hypnotic spell cast by the profound stillness of the vast West Valley. Black hawks soared above the rugged cliffs that framed the silent gorge, home of five dead pharaohs. The only disturbance breaking the eerie hush of loneliness was a swirl of dust raised by the vehicle. Surry felt a surge of elation as if he were returning home.

Bradford Dunn and Roxy Morgan had arrived at the project site earlier that morning and were diligently arranging equipment near the mouth of Amenhotep's tomb. Dunn, a retired surveyor, was living a lifetime dream by using his surveying skills in royal tombs. It was his fourth season with the professor and the wiry perfectionist continued to be a welcomed asset to the team, both for his surveying expertise and his generous contributions to the Arizona Expedition Fund.

Roxy, the young doctoral candidate of Middle Eastern Studies, had enough stamina to handle the combined duties of official photographer, research assistant, and documentation manager. The skills of the energetic blonde served the team well, as did the welcomed donations from her wealthy father.

The local workers that Surry requested had been dutifully rounded up by Ali, a loyal Muslim who had worked for years with the Arizona team. An eight-week job assignment at seven dollars a day could support a worker's family for nearly a year, which made collecting a crew of local natives an easy task. Ali had proved his honesty as foreman of the native team, taking responsibility for the weekly pay envelopes and the organization of work schedules.

The band of gowned men rose from their squatting circle of rising cigarette smoke and approached the Professor and his wife with handshakes and introductions. The group was chattering and grinning, well aware that they were among the lucky few to be employed during the disastrous downturn in local tourism.

Valerie approached Bradford Dunn with a friendly hug. She had grown to admire the modest gray-haired man for his willingness to donate his time and skills. Roxy bounded toward the professor and his wife, welcoming her mentors with warm girlish embraces. Her spontaneous friendliness obviously intrigued the Egyptian men who were unaccustomed to conspicuous female expressiveness. More than once Roxy's jovial gestures were misinterpreted in Egypt as an invitation for romance. In the past two summers spent with the Semaines she had learn to subdue her good-natured personality which Arab men found particularly fascinating when it came from a full-bodied blonde.

The group was eager to get started with the new season of work, but they managed to sit in quiet attention while Dr. Semaine outlined specific goals of the summer assignment. Surry used simple English terms when speaking to the native workmen. Most of the older men understood English surprisingly well after years of associating with Westerners. Surry was aware of the importance of loyalty and respect among Muslim work teams and was able to deal sensitively with their customs and sense of dignity.

The eight-man crew had trudged to the West Valley across the nearby hills that very morning on a steep path with the sifters, mallets, baskets, shovels and picks that were left with the foreman for safekeeping from the previous season's expedition. Bradford Dunn kept his surveying tools separate and insisted on taking care of his own delicate instruments in one of Luxor's rental sheds.

The first week's assignment consisted of shoring up unsafe support pillars in the passageways of Amenhotep's tomb and the verification of last season's measurements. The second week's agenda called for a more interesting schedule, when work in the deeper areas of the crumbling tomb could begin.

Surry informed the team that maps indicated an additional storeroom somewhere inside the tomb and that he hoped for new findings during the work period. Surry skipped lightly over information concerning the "lost storeroom" mentioning only that an old sketch of the tomb showed a small alcove which may have been a hiding place for more funeral goods. The laborers were mainly interested in the daily assignments of sifting and sorting and, above all, the weekly pay envelope. They paid little attention to the detailed explanations about the overall explorations.

Roxy was elated with the prospect of uncovering one of Amenhotep's sealed storerooms. It usually took years for younger colleagues to be accepted in the world of senior savants; however, belonging to a team that made a significant discovery could accelerate one's prestige in academic circles. At sixty-five, Bradford Dunn was open for any new experience that would keep his life meaningful. He sought no more than that.

What the Semaines truly had in mind for the penetration of the south wall would have electrified the senses of both Bradford and Roxy. For the moment, Blumfield's map that Surry had in his possession was not a matter that he or Valerie could discuss with anyone this early. The complete work program that Dr. Semaine had submitted to the Antiquities Council had no reference of another tomb in the vicinity. The current permit did not allow for a major incision in the walls of Amenhotep's burial place, only a minor invasion to probe for a rumored storeroom. Since arriving in the Sahara, the Semaines were careful not to mention the name Herihor, except in whispered tones between themselves.

Deceiving the Egyptian Supreme Antiquities Council for the first time in Surry's career played havoc with his conscience. Addictions have been known to lure men to foul play—even high-minded men—and Surry was an incurable addict when it came to Pharaonic treasures.

Inspector Rachid unlocked the chain on the tomb's gated entrance which held the metal sign marked "CLOSED TO THE PUBLIC." With an air of authority, he pushed the rusty metal bars inward toward the cool dark tunnel and motioned the group to follow the beam of his laser light until he switched on the string of small electric bulbs left from other years of probing.

Even at eight in the morning, heat was building up in the rocky terrain, making the workers impatient to enter the shelter of the dark cave; however, it was not the comfort of the coolness that drew Surry, Valerie, Brad and Roxy down the irregular steps of the shadowy passageway. For those passionate about ancient civilizations, entering a three-thousand-year-old structure which weeps of lost magnificence is exhilarating.

The carefully-hewn plaster walls of the passage gave evidence of artisans from centuries long ago. Traces of colored pigment which had survived thousands of years still clung to the crumbling carvings which lined the sloping downward route. The uneven glow from the crude string of lights along the path outlined the shadows of the slow moving group. The professor and the inspector scrutinized the ceiling supports for fresh fissures that might warn of new weaknesses. Project leaders had the responsibility to see that tombs were safe for exploration and were not a trap that might further populate the world of the dead. The minor rockslides along the way did not alarm the experienced excavators who were on the lookout for more serious structural damage. The inspector appeared satisfied that the corridor was safe enough. He gave his approval for the season to officially begin.

As the group continued down the uneven walkway, Surry stayed behind momentarily to step into a miniature funerary chapel to calm the quiver within his chest. Beginning a new season in the underground world of the pharaohs was always a thrill for Surry Semaine and he paused to record the moment of joy firmly in his mind.

Valerie, too, relished the return to the mystical surroundings; however, her emotion was driven more by the obvious euphoria that gripped the man she loved. When she followed Surry into the small hushed prayer room where he stood motionless, the charged atmosphere made her shiver. She remained silent until her husband turned around and whispered, "We're lucky people, Val."

Valerie smiled with a knowing nod and reached for his hand.

CHAPTER 9

While sorting through debris left from the previous season, several funerary fragments of interest came to light. Excitement ran high when a small dirt-encrusted lapis cobra head showed up among the broken rocks in the corner of the main burial chamber. When layers of dust were carefully brushed from the miniature item, the gold-rimmed eyes of the blue serpent stared out.

Aside from the delicate beauty of the article, it had particular significance due to the similarity of the larger serpent head found mounted on King Tutankhamen's solid gold mummy mask. It gave further evidence that Amenhotep III had been buried with similar masks of gold, stolen long ago by invaders. It was conceivable that hasty tomb robbers carelessly discarded the broken serpent, not realizing—nor caring—about the historical significance of the tiny object. The amount of precious metal contained in the snakehead had minimal value to hassled invaders, but to Dr. Semaine the item was worthy of an entire page of notes in his journal.

Other finds of interest surfaced during the following

days, including a broken figure representing a servant to the king in his underworld existence. Faience *shabti* statues which were images of humans who assisted the dead king, were becoming exceedingly rare after the rush of dealers marketing the figures as "precious tomb treasures."

Precious bits and pieces of burial items gathered by the team in the beginning days of the dig were photographed, labeled, wrapped in cotton and placed in a locked metal case belonging to the Egyptian inspector. New government policies required all man-made fragments from the royal necropolis to be examined by the Antiquities Council. Restoration experts had become astute at filling in museum sculptures with missing chips that turned up in the ongoing excavations of noble tombs.

Uncovering these precious morsels in the tomb of Amenhotep occupied the team for several days; nevertheless, the urge to invade the nearby wall indicated in Blumfield's sketch was ever-present on Surry's mind. He managed to find time alone each day to secretly examine portions of the wall in the tomb's first pillared room to locate an ideal spot to make an incision into the limestone.

A curious surprise jolted the Semaines during the second week on the site. While they were photographing the faded hieroglyphs in the antechamber of the burial vault, Rachid approached to announce that an American female was at the tomb entrance demanding to speak to the project leader. Exchanging puzzled glances, Surry and Val trudged up the rocky tunnel of the tomb.

Usually if one bothered to take the four-mile detour to the lesser-known West Valley, the visitor was taken to the restored tomb of Ay, the pharaoh who reigned after Tutankhamen. The trail that led to the ruined tomb of Amenhotep III was barely visible from the main gravel road and the worn sign with the words "CLOSED FOR RESTORATION" discouraged tourists. Few foreigners had the audacity to venture into the forbidding crevices of the West Valley's towering hills.

Adjusting their eyes to the sunlight, Surry and Val spotted an attractive woman dressed in a crisp cotton pantsuit leaning against a late model Mercedes. A long-limbed native driver stood nearby studying the arid surroundings.

When the new arrival caught sight of the approaching professor, she dropped her cigarette, grinding it out with the heel of a stylish boot. Disregarding Valerie's presence, the visitor reached out to shake hands with the professor.

"Doctor Semaine, I presume," she said with a wry smile. "I'm Joan Kaufman, a friend of Charles Blumfield. He mentioned that you might be willing to show me your restoration project while I'm staying in Luxor…hope I'm not disturbing you at a critical time."

Surry shot a perplexed look to Val, who coolly eyed the newcomer. "This is my wife, Valerie, who assists with the project. Unfortunately, due to the dangers involved, it's not possible to take visitors into the tomb. We would need a permit from the Antiquities Council. How long will you be in town?"

"I'll be at the Winter Palace for a month on an assignment for a travel magazine. Egypt's current low rates have allowed me to take some extra time here. Charles told me you might be helpful and I would adore seeing your work. I hope you can arrange a visit." The lighthearted goodbye uttered by Joan Kaufman as she turned toward the waiting sedan did not lift the heaviness of the scene.

Surry turned away, struggling to make sense of the irritating encounter. He and Val remained silent until they were within the protective walls of the tomb.

"Shit!" fumed Surry when he could no longer contain his agitation. "All we need is one of Blumfield's lackeys spying on us. Just like him to pull this!"

"We don't know for sure," soothed Valerie, "but it's curious that Miss Kaufman knew exactly how to find us. Hanging out in the desert in the middle of summer doesn't fit that girl's style."

"Damn good thing we haven't broken into that wall yet," Surry fumed. "That's probably what Blumfield wants to know. Little Joanie isn't going to have much of a report if and when she gets in here."

Valerie gently slipped her hand in his as they made their way in the passageway of the tomb. The firm squeeze she gave Surry's damp palm relayed more than words. She knew the waiting hieroglyphs would pacify her husband's agitation.

CHAPTER 10

Joan Kaufman walked confidently through the carved doors of the grand old Winter Palace Hotel. The doors were held open by two bronze-skinned doormen dressed in billowing red pasha pants and embroidered white silk blouses. On the head of each burly man was a tasseled black fez. The desk manager greeted Joan from behind a mahogany reception counter located near the entrance of the enormous lobby.

Thick Persian rugs covered most of the marble floor and under each giant Venetian glass chandelier was a group of comfortable cushioned divans waiting for guests to sit and observe the activity taking place among the affluent visitors. Joan's long, shapely legs easily climbed the palatial staircase to her second-floor suite overlooking the Nile River.

Although Joan's intimate relationship with Blumfield had cooled during the past few years, she had not severed business ties with him. His offer to send her to Luxor to scout out the activities of Professor Semaine sounded intriguing at a time when she needed a break from the Beverly Hills crowd. Charles offered a generous expense account and relaxing accommodations at the Winter Palace

47

at a convenient time for Joan, who was ready for new scenery. Charles knew her well enough to appeal to her sense of adventure.

In many ways, Joan was a loner, entertained by her own imagination, while Blumfield enjoyed controlling other people's lives. In the past, their clever schemes and pranks had been considered more mischievous than downright malicious; however, the current plot of Joan's former lover elevated the game to higher stakes. The possibility of priceless treasures made the two friends willing to dabble in danger.

Joan's knowledge of Egyptian history was more significant than the impression she had conveyed to the Semaines. Her degree in Eastern Cultures and numerous field trips in North African countries made Joan an ideal choice to take on the covert scouting assignment. It was the sort of intrigue that suited the restless thirty-seven-year-old woman as she approached middle age.

The cool shower spray running down Joan's back was refreshing. The shiny gold fixtures and marble-lined bathroom had been luxuriously updated since the old hotel's heyday in the late 1800's when it served as a winter playground for rich Europeans.

Joan was satisfied that she had managed to make a connection with Surry Semaine, as brief as it was. She decided to reward herself with a swim and a leisurely poolside lunch in the hotel's palm tree-lined botanical garden before calling California later that afternoon.

Professor Semaine called Joan two days later telling her that he was able to arrange a visit to Amenhotep's tomb on Friday, which was the crew's holy day off. Only a few Christian Arabs worked on Fridays. The small crew at the tomb had been on the job for several hours when Ali alerted

Semaine that a visitor had arrived.

Surry approached the woman with reserved politeness. "Good morning," he muttered, noting the expensive camera hanging from her shoulder. "I'll have to ask you to leave your camera in the car, Miss Kaufman. The university reserves exclusive rights to photograph inside the tomb."

Joan obediently handed the camera to her driver. It had been worth a try. Surry watched Joan's sure-footed descent down the hazardous stairs in the shadowy tunnel. She followed the path of her guide's flashlight with her own laser beam as they crossed the improvised wooden plank across the deep well shaft, a forbidding hole often dug out in eighteenth-dynasty tombs to discourage tomb robbers.

"The sights get better the deeper we go," whispered Surry, the usual tone he used in the sanctified surroundings. "The images are a bit brighter as we near the burial chamber. The first level of the tomb appears unfinished."

The tomb map that Charles had sketched for Joan was fixed in her mind and she nonchalantly scanned the first pillared hall with her flashlight, avoiding any sign that it was of special interest. The ten-by-ten-foot room, designed to look like an abandoned burial chamber, ended with a roughly-hewn stone wall at the far end built to camouflage the opening of the tunnel leading to the actual burial chamber which had contained Amenhotep's massive sarcophagus.

Professional tomb robbers quickly became shrewd about deceptive barriers and they often burrowed through limestone walls in search of secret passages leading to hidden riches. Ancient criminal records indicate that most of the royal tombs were robbed in antiquity by gangs who paid corrupt construction workers to acquire information about the configurations of tombs they had helped build.

After Jean-Francois Champollion, the son of a poor French bookseller, decoded the hieroglyphs from the Rosetta Stone in 1822, papyrus scrolls dating from fourteenth century B.C. court records were translated telling of trials ending in the executions of numerous men involved in tomb robberies. Today in the Cairo Egyptian Museum one can see three-thousand-year-old papyri listing the names of tomb invaders and details of their interrogations and punishments, as well as the booty recovered and the task of resealing a disturbed tomb.

The persistent pilferage of the giant pyramids near Cairo caused later pharaohs to become more secretive about the location of their tombs. By 1660 B.C., Egyptian rulers began building their final resting places far from Cairo in the remote valley near Thebes, a village now known as Luxor. Artisans who worked on royal tombs were often blindfolded by foremen on the route to a sacred burial site. If their loyalty was in question they were put to death. Few barriers can deter the human drive from greed and, sadly, the ruthless plunder of the royal tombs continues to the present day.

Robbers in the pharaonic era were primarily interested in metal of any type, preferably gold or silver. The next most desirable loot was ivory, glass, jewelry and chests packed with the king's afterlife wardrobe. Perfumes, cosmetics, wines and oils were highly prized and brought a high price if recovered shortly after the precious supplies were placed in the burial chamber and were still in a state of usefulness. Recorded evidence of tomb break-ins within the first few years after a noble funeral reinforces the theory that the invasions and plunder were carried out by dishonest tomb laborers.

King Tutankhamen's tomb was entered twice by thieves

during the first several years following his death. In both cases the bandits were apprehended and brutally carted off by guards while officials hurriedly piled up the disturbed funerary objects in the first room of the small tomb. The door blockings were then resealed by high priests and the stairway leading down to Tut's burial chamber was filled with heavy rocks, sand and rubble to discourage future villains. Construction on the tomb of Rameses VI began shortly after Tut's burial and the debris from the digging of a new tomb was also piled on the entrance of Tut's resting place, which stayed hidden for over three thousand years.

A dirt road built for tourists in the early twentieth century contributed even more debris in the vicinity of Tut's tomb, leaving the historic treasures underground in a state of darkness until 1922. The English archaeologist, Howard Carter, uncovered a rough step near the roadway in November, 1922. He immediately updated his permit to dig further and soon came upon a sealed wooden door leading into the room filled with the long-lost funerary treasures of Tutankhamen. This spectacular discovery has continued to fascinate the civilized world for the past century.

Considering that ancient hieroglyphs indicate Amenhotep III was one of the wealthiest pharaohs of the 18th dynasty, historians tend to agree that his burial objects would have been many times greater than that of the young King Tutankhamen. It is mind-boggling to estimate the riches of Amenhotep that have been carried off and dispersed by thieves in the 3300 years since his mummy was placed in his vast tomb.

Professor Semaine's mission in Amenhotep's tomb was to document the faded hieroglyphs that had not yet been translated. At least that was what the professor's current permit indicated. Valerie and Surry had been content for years with publishing translations of temple and tomb writings, but no matter how involved an archaeologist may be in historical data, discovering a forgotten tomb remains an elusive dream. Blumfield's map fanned the smoldering flames forever lingering in Surry's imagination.

Joan Kaufman followed closely behind Surry as he led her downward to another set of crude steps into the decorated antechamber where Valerie was intently copying the wall carvings which portrayed Amenhotep's presentation to "the deities of the underworld" before his sarcophagus entered its final chamber.

Valerie gave no sign of welcoming the woman accompanying her husband. She didn't like the intruder's looks nor did she trust Joan's intentions. The visitor, in her freshly pressed khakis, blond hair, manicured nails and baby-fine skin, did not belong in the musty air of the sepulcher, which Valerie considered privileged territory.

Valerie murmured a dutiful greeting, barely raising her head from the notebook in her hand. Remaining in the shadows, Valerie discouraged further conversation. Likewise, Joan showed little interest in Surry's wife. Surry led the way into the majestic six-pillared burial sanctuary of Amenhotep III.

The cool-mannered woman was not prepared for the sense of timelessness and profound silence that engulfed her as she stepped into the shadowy vault. The royal chamber radiated an aura of elegance despite vandalism and careless intruders of the past. The lofty arch of the star-studded ceiling, the stately pillars and the painted walls jolted even jaded souls to a level of astonishment when seen for the first time.

The thick limestone pillars retained discernible images of figures kneeling in homage to Osiris, the God of the

Underworld. What was left of brightly painted walls were only remnants of the vivid blues, greens, ruby reds, and gold made from mineral dyes that were still impressive to the eye even though artisans had applied their art three thousand years ago. Except the damage done by vandals and the chopped-out chunks of wall art taken by more recent scavengers, what was left of the exquisite carvings had been preserved by the dryness of the desert and the darkness of the crypt. First-time tourists to Egypt are incredulous and often unable to believe that the polychrome figures in many of the tombs have not been touched-up.

Minutes passed while Surry and the visitor stood enveloped in the solemn hush of the noble space. Surry entered this sacred vault often, but the impact of reverence never failed to engulf him in the ghostly presence of a dead king "whose word alone was sufficient to make the world tremble."

All that remained of the actual grave goods that once filled Amenhotep's richly-prepared crypt were broken fragments of the enormous red granite sarcophagus, which had been removed by ancient officials—evidently to be used in another noble burial. During the heightened era of tomb heists, the linen-wrapped mummy of Amenhotep had been removed from its coffin by priests for safe-keeping in a secret hiding place. Carelessly left behind were colored shards of man-made offerings, chunks of red granite, wreckage and debris.

Joan slowly circled the quiet chamber, her eyes riveted on the cobalt-blue ceiling dotted with gold stars. She dared to run her fingers along the fine etchings chiseled on the walls. "Thank you for taking the time to show me this, Doctor Semaine." Joan's tone was quietly respectful, her usual arrogance subdued.

Her obvious admiration for what she had seen pacified Surry's initial contempt for the woman. Perhaps he had been mistaken about her motives for coming to Luxor; nonetheless her association with Blumfield was irksome and Surry was wary.

"What about that room over there?" she asked, stepping toward a narrow door in one corner of the chamber. Her easygoing persistence was difficult to refuse, although Surry now decided that Joan was overstaying her welcome.

Surry reluctantly led the woman into the small adjoining room. "Amenhotep commissioned two separate spaces to hold the remains of his favorite wives, Tiye and Sitamun. These wives probably outlived him and historians believe the priests opposed unsealing the King's tomb for their burials, so they were buried somewhere else," remarked Surry, pointing out fragments of hieroglyphs honoring Queen Tiye. "There are many details about the royal families we may never know."

"Makes me want to do my homework," whispered Joan, breathing in the stuffy air. "It's been fascinating...I've loved being here."

Surry's annoyance with the interruption of his workday subsided somewhat as he found himself observing Joan's lithe figure striding up the passageway. Her pale clear skin was a pleasant change among the sunbaked Egyptians and her polished appearance added a glow to the dusty surroundings. The impulse that stirred within him was a brief reminder that he still belonged to the land of the living, an unfamiliar reaction during his underworld probes.

Barely looking up from her sketches, Valerie nodded with a forced smile as Surry and Joan climbed toward the tunnel entrance. "Good riddance," she whispered to herself.

That evening, the lone waiter hurriedly turned on the

overhead fan when Surry and Valerie walked into the dining area of the Nefertari Hotel. Their order was the same as always—the rice and vegetable plate which they knew was the safest offering on the menu. Discussing Joan Kaufman proceeded to spice up the bland dinner.

"Just can't get a fix on what's up with that lady," Surry said idly. "Can you?"

"You're the one who spent so much time with her. You should be able to figure it out." Valerie's displeasure was evident.

"Well, she's not the bimbo I had her pegged for. She's familiar with antiquities and seems to have a genuine interest in history. She didn't ask too many questions, so maybe her story about the travel assignment is on the level. Maybe we're just touchy because of the Blumfield connection,"

"Perhaps, but I hope she doesn't make a habit of dropping in on us."

"That's for sure. We break into that wall next week and we sure as hell don't want anyone nosing around then." Surry's voice sounded prickly. The mere thought of what might be waiting in the West Valley gave his pulse a rush.

"It's your call who's allowed on the site. Blumfield can't get into the country, so he'll have to settle for what we tell him and his little spy can keep her distance!"

"True. Let's steer clear of Miss Kaufman. We're not tour guides and there's too much at stake to lose focus now!" But the lady in question was not as easy to get rid of as Surry thought. He was correct in recognizing that Joan Kaufman was not a bimbo.

CHAPTER 11

To this day, Egyptian workers continue to be superstitious about curses connected with sacred shrines, making the process of disrupting tomb walls a sensitive undertaking. Instructing an Egyptian crew to sift and carry out debris from an already violated tomb was a routine matter, but Professor Semaine found that the act of mutilating a solid tomb wall was problematic for the natives.

Three trusted crew members were selected to work on the secretive assignment. Surry informed the official inspector that he had secured approval to search for a royal storeroom that was rumored to be nearby. The professor's easy manner paid off and he managed to persuade the three workers to begin chipping into the wall of the first pillared room.

Valerie and Surry reviewed the Egyptian Museum's ancient descriptions of Herihor's funeral cortege and then compared Blumfield's map of the lost tomb with various other historic papyrus that related to royal tombs in the West Valley. Considering that the nearby Valley of the Kings was crammed with over fifty known tombs, it seemed logical that the princely burial grounds would have been extended into the adjacent West Valley. It was realistic to presume that the vast West Valley Canyon held more tombs than the five that had been discovered and documented on current published maps. Somewhere in this barren valley, Surry Semaine was determined to find Herihor.

The prospect of further discoveries in the lonely West Valley was not a new idea among Egyptologists. Giovanni Belzoni, the eccentric Italian explorer, had combed the cliff walls in the nineteenth century with remarkable success even though he worked with primitive equipment. From 1815 to 1820 the Italian adventurer unearthed the unfinished and unused tomb of Akhenaton, who was the controversial ruler believed to be King Tut's father. Generally, twentieth century archaeologists concentrated on the better known tombs in the Valley of the Kings, especially after Howard Carter's sensational discovery of King Tutankhamen in 1922.

When the news of King Tut's golden treasures flashed in the global media frenzy, the number of fortune hunters skyrocketed and the Egyptian government hurriedly placed strict controls on foreigners coming to dig for pharaonic artifacts. Valid excavation permits suddenly became more difficult to secure and treasure hunting along the Nile River was no longer the open-sport it had been prior to Carter's discovery of Tut. Even native tomb robbers had to carry out their illegal trade in a more cautious manner, as customs officers became more organized about detecting the source of ancient collectibles on the black market.

Professor Semaine was one of the fortunate archaeologists whose untarnished reputation and generous university budget allowed his projects in Egypt to continue. Surry was not only a trusted scholar, but he had a talent for raising funds which was an important income for the Egyptian Minister of Culture. While many American, French and Japanese academic teams managed to remain on good terms with Egyptian authorities in the early twentieth century, the arrogance of some English and German explorers often caused their exploration permits to be temporarily denied.

After the debacle Charles Blumfield had brought upon himself at the Egyptian Museum, Surry and Val were acutely aware of preserving their own academic reputations in the competitive world of archaeologists. Merely being associated with a rogue like Blumfield was a gamble; nevertheless, a lead concerning Herihor was too tempting to resist. The fixation on adventure often clouds a person's good judgment.

Surry's puritan upbringing was not easily derailed. Blumfield's devious scheme bothered Surry, often interrupting his sleep with villainous images. Even his daydreams were occupied with rationalizations, telling himself that a sensational find would rekindle Egypt's distressed tourism industry and ultimately justify the devious process. One could only imagine what treasures a man like Charles Blumfield would ferret away if he had the opportunity, but Surry was determined to keep the project respectable. It was common knowledge that even the most ethical archaeologists had the tendency to pocket a few small mementoes from historic graveside digs.

The first puncture into the side wall of Amenhotep's tomb was executed by Surry himself. Measurements for the 3-foot-by-4-foot tunnel required accuracy in directing the angle toward the hollow area shown on Blumfield's drawing. The wall selected was undecorated, easing Surry's conscience as his mallet broke into the limestone with the traditional wood and metal tools. The intense work of chipping stone may have been tedious for most people. For Surry Semaine the mere hint of locating the lost king produced an energetic drive forward.

In ancient times, construction on the tomb of a reigning Pharaoh began the first year after a new king's coronation. Grandiose tombs could take decades of treacherous work to dig out and decorate according to the strict traditions. Often a royal burial place would be incomplete if the king died early in his reign as is obvious in the small, cramped space where the nineteen-year-old Tutankhamen was placed following the abrupt burial after his unexpected death. He had been on the throne for less than a decade.

Upon the death of a ruling monarch, workers had to complete a royal tomb the best they could before the customary 70-day mourning period ended when the mummified king was ready to be transported to his underworld dwelling. Even though Amenhotep III had been in power for 38 years, artisans were still busy at work on his elaborate tomb when his death was announced. It was evident that the upper walls of the tomb had not been finished leaving several areas near the entrance only sparely adorned. Fortunately for Surry, chipping through the wall he had chosen to work on did not mar any markings. Many Egyptian workers would have walked off the job if they saw the destruction of sacred images.

By noon of the fourth day, Surry and two workers had the outline of a crawl space burrowed several feet into the limestone. Surry calculated that it would take nearly a month of diligent work to hack a tunnel near the spot indicated on Blumfield's map.

The furtive project was carried on with minimum discussion, as if it were merely a task to locate a minor storeroom. As long as the crew working on Amenhotep's tomb was paid and did not run out of cigarettes or disturb sacred symbols, there was little concern what when on during the daily work routine.

The leisurely pace of daily commerce in Luxor became even more sluggish during the hot summer months. Tempers smoldered, pettiness increased and competition for passengers heated up among the local carriage drivers. The tourist trade which the town depended upon was at a discouraging level due to current terrorist activities, leaving only a few audacious travelers to take advantage of reduced hotel rates. Religious extremists aimed for visitor centers where violence would produce the most international media coverage and would cause the most disruption and fear.

Restaurants and hotels in Luxor were desperate for business and recent falling prices allowed the meager budget of the University of Arizona archaeological team to enjoy better eating establishments. One evening, when the team splurged on dinner at the posh Winter Palace Hotel, Valerie and Surry spotted Joan Kaufman.

Joan nonchalantly sauntered into the hotel's dignified Victoria Bar looking cool and stylish in a mint-green *jelabiya* with ropes of amber beads swinging around her neck. The thin cotton gown framed a provocative shadow of the shapely figure beneath. Valerie noticed the admiring glances of Bradford and Surry as Joan glided toward their table. Suddenly, Valerie felt an awkward dissatisfaction with her own plain skirt and loose fitting blouse.

"We like your posh dwelling, Miss Kaufman. Must be nice to camp out here," greeted Bradford cheerfully. "How's your writing going?" The surveyor was eager to strike up a friendly conversation with the attractive lady, unaware of Surry's suspicions.

"I like this hotel. It feels peaceful and safe. I've been able to get a lot of work done. Mind if I join you?" Valerie sat tight-lipped while Bradford got up and pulled another chair to the corner table. Surry refrained from showing any encouragement.

Welcoming a fresh face to the foursome was fine with Roxy. There were so few Americans in Luxor this season and conversation with Arab men was not encouraged for a young Western blonde. Not many Arab women were seen in public except to shop at the town's open market.

"Not much action around here is there?" injected Roxy. "What do you do for fun?"

"My driver is good about showing me the sights. We take a drive in the morning. After that I stay in and write during hot afternoons. The place can get lonely so it's nice to see friends like you. I usually don't leave the hotel in the evening."

"Sounds like us," smiled Roxy. "We have to be in the field by five in the morning."

"May I buy you all a drink?" Joan offered as she requested a gin and tonic when the waiter approached. "You were so kind to welcome me on the site. I hope to see it again sometime."

Bradford felt compelled to break the awkward silence following Joan's comment. "What do you say, chief, are we allowed to have more visitors?"

"Plenty busy now, but we'll see how the schedule goes. Perhaps we can arrange time for Miss Kaufman later on." Surry strained to sound sincere.

Valerie caught Surry's sidelong look. Joan Kaufman was hanging around Luxor longer than necessary for a simple magazine article. *For God's sake mind your own business, bitch,* thought Val, as she sipped her wine and attempted to curtail the conversation.

CHAPTER 12

The following week the small crew hit a mass of flint in the secretive passageway, forcing a laborious detour around the stubborn outcropping of white stone. The three workmen systematically carried the chips out of the cavity in primitive wicker baskets. Debris was strategically scattered in surrounding crevices in an effort to avoid notice of unusual digging activity.

Bradford and Roxy were curious, but carried on with their assignments. They had seen the Semaines on fervent tangents in the past and knew enough not to pester the couple until more details about the royal storeroom was discussed openly.

The dense flint mound took several days to circumvent before the compass again pointed in the designated direction outlined by the map, but a significant revelation soon made up for the disappointing delay. During the third week of burrowing, Surry's hands trembled when his density meter suddenly registered a hollow space looming ahead. He and Valerie forced themselves to appear calm during the rest of the morning until the workmen left in the afternoon when they could verify the meter reading more carefully.

"The void continues to register." Surry's heart beat quickened. "Maybe it's a natural fault, but there's something curious ahead. It's late. Let's go back to town and think this over. We can push further tomorrow."

Doing their best to contain themselves, the professor and his wife carried on routinely the following day. Surry was lifting a basket of shale to carry out when he saw one of the trusted workmen back out of the crawl space wide-eyed and panting.

"Bad omen in there," gasped the superstitious native. "No more digging."

"It's probably an air pocket, Ashid. I'll check it out. Take a break, while I go in," answered Surry coolly.

Surry's flashlight bounced along the jagged walls of the narrow passage. At the end of the stuffy space, Surry pushed away a pile of rubble and tapped a rocky wall with his hammer. A faint echo quivered back at him. A chill evaporated the perspiration forming on the back of his neck. As his imagination soared, he forgot that he had left Val anxiously waiting.

He feverishly aimed a slender hand-held drill into the rock barrier. When the metal tool jerked forward as if a phantom from the other side had yanked at it, Surry felt queasy and his pores oozed a clammy sweat. He grasped at the oxygen hose beside him, trying to soothe his palpitating heart. A feeble hiss of putrid, dry air wheezed toward him when he pulled the drill from the tiny hole. Surry remained motionless for an indeterminable period before slowly crawling back to the chamber where Valerie sat near the opening of the crawlspace. She had excused the two workers to smoke outside.

"What's going on in there? You were quiet for so long!"

"There's an echo all right," mumbled Surry, nervously brushing off his pants. "Could be signs of a cave-in or something a lot more interesting. Can't tell yet." He seemed confused and remained vague as he noticed Bradford and Roxy enter the chamber on their way out for a break in open air.

The two associates were not yet privy to the grandiose schemes of Charles Blumfield, but they both sensed the exhilaration bursting from Surry and Val as they passed them in the dim room. Bradford had assumed there was a bigger explanation than looking for a simple storeroom that warranted such a deep break-in; however, his questions had been put off with hazy answers. It was time to pin down their leader for the whole story.

A blanket of heavy heat enveloped the four Americans as they trudged into the open air. The sun was at its midday peak and the Egyptian crew had already piled into the flatbed truck heading down the winding road toward the workers' village beyond the West Valley.

"Let's head to the hotel for a shower, Brad. We'll meet you for dinner and discuss some new developments." Surry sensed Brad's inquisitive gaze; however, it was not yet time to answer questions when his thoughts were too jumbled to converse clearly. Valerie and Surry jumped into the jeep, while Brad and Roxy waited for the inspector to lock the tomb entrance for the night.

As Valerie entered the stifling hotel room, she switched on the noisy cooler. Surry headed directly for the sink, splashing his face with water. He had managed to control outward signs of exhilaration until he was safely within the privacy of their room.

"My God, Val, I think we're on to something! I could feel it, smell it...gave me the shivers."

"You think the map might be right?" probed Valerie, pulling off her grimy boots. "We've got to stay cool if something's really there. Dealing with Blumfield will be dicey. I don't trust the man."

"Let's see what's beyond that wall before we get crazed. It's time we let Brad and Roxy in on the matter. They're getting suspicious and deserve to know what we're up to."

Valerie lay on the bed starring at the ceiling. "You're right, they can be trusted, but for now let's say the passageway is too unstable for anyone except you. You've got to be the first to see if anything is really there."

"Actually, the cave-in danger is real, especially if there's a sizable cavity somewhere near. It's eerie in there. Good thing I'm not claustrophobic."

"Well, I'm smaller than you, maybe I should be first to poke through," Valerie offered with a smirk.

"No way! You'll see soon enough, when I find out it's safe."

"Oh, sure, you'd be livid if I laid eyes on that pile of gold first."

"Glad you're convinced there's gold waiting for us." He leaned over and brushed her cheek with a kiss. "Let's go to dinner and plot how to handle fame and fortune."

CHAPTER 13

Few souls craved fame more than Charles Blumfield. He could afford the material pleasures and comforts he desired, but had not managed to buy respect and glory among his peers. Dutiful attention from his financial advisors was not enough to satisfy him. The few hours he spent each morning managing a list of investments no longer kept him satisfied. Lately, Charles was far more fascinated with the venture he was involved with in Egypt.

He dialed the Winter Palace Hotel each night from his San Francisco apartment in time to wake Joan in Luxor. Anticipating the daily phone call from Charles did not give Joan the same thrill it used to before their affair had come to an end years ago. There was a time when Joan had allowed herself to become emotionally dependent on the attractive playboy, wanting more from him than his married status and self-indulgence would allow.

Charles had been able to compensate for Joan's stress over the clandestine relationship by giving her favors and gifts. Joan appreciated the trendy loft near San Francisco's new library and the sporty Mercedes that Charles provided.

However, when Joan dined alone on her thirty-fourth birthday, she vowed to look for a more suitable companion who could be seen with her in public. Being involved with a married man is not satisfactory for a lady who likes to spend holidays and cozy Saturday nights with the one she loves.

As for Charles, he was not interested in altering his comfortable lifestyle. The balance of an acceptable family arrangement, enviable assets, social status and sexual diversity suited him just fine. He had no intention of jeopardizing his financial situation and satisfactory lifestyle with the needs of others.

Years ago, Joan braced herself and made the break, leaving San Francisco to take a position in Los Angeles with Conde Nast. The bayside condo that had been given to her was quickly leased to an interior designer and Charles was left behind to find a new playmate. Not one to grovel for favors, Blumfield gave up after telephoning Joan for weeks after her departure. His flirtations with Wall Street, women and Egyptian antiquities were there to fill the void and there was no shortage of money to spend on newly-found frolics.

Although money had a powerful voice in California, the tone was different in Egypt. Charles had failed to bribe his way out of the botched fiasco at the Egyptian Museum, where he was still considered an undesirable visitor. He had been unceremoniously ushered out of Egypt with the border slammed shut. He did not intend to be banished forever from the Land of the Pharaohs, especially now when he possessed a clue to undiscovered riches. The challenge to pursue Herihor in a country where he was not welcome made the game all the more challenging.

"It appears that progress is being made in Tomb 22, Charles," purred Joan on the phone. "The team seems to be busy on the site, but no one knows much about it. My driver's cousin is on the work crew and passes through a room where a small tunnel has been started, but that's all he's able to gather. I've paid the man to keep his eyes open and his mouth shut."

"Good work. What about you? Are you able to visit the site again?" Blumfield inquired, gazing at the lights on the Golden Gate Bridge from his high-rise apartment building.

"The Semaines are not that friendly and they haven't invited me back. I can tell they're not eager to have me around. Their assistant, Roxy, likes me; at least I'm making headway with her."

"Try to take a look. Something's brewing. The professor was evasive when I called him. He's a fairly straight shooter, but a big find could alter his ethics about our agreement."

"Between Fatime and his cousin, we have an idea about the work at the site, but no details about what's going on in that new tunnel. I'll try to snoop around tomorrow."

"Stay with it, girl. Call me when you return to the hotel."

Surry Semaine cautiously chipped on the limestone at the end of the eerie crawl space. The lantern captured his cautious moves in the shadows while the stale air that breathed toward him from the tiny puncture blurred his senses. It was a delicate odor, not unpleasant, but musty and strange—different from anything Surry had ever encountered.

Surry was oblivious to the perspiration dripping from his damp hair, unconcerned about his cramped muscles and unaware of his pounding heart. Carefully enlarging the tiny peek hole with a wooden tool, he proceeded to press his eye to the gritty wall. His eyes were barely able to distinguish the conditions beyond the sharp beam of the laser light strapped to his head.

Details on the other side of the barrier gradually took

shape through the shadows, while the professor crouched rigidly, stupefied by the faint outline that came into focus. The narrow beam of light reflected upon decorated walls, furniture, jars, cabinets, stacks of boxes, and various large and small statues. Surry glared at an immense sarcophagus in the cavern's center. Although it appeared that the massive stone lid had been set askew—no doubt by early invaders— most of what he could see seemed orderly.

He was motionless as he stared at the magnificent clutter. Time for him was nonexistent as he reached a level of euphoria that was burned in his memory neurons, a sensation he wanted to remember forever, even if it meant it would be his last vision on earth. His imagination magically reached out to the ghostly chamber allowing his senses to feel the gauzy linen coverings, to smell the oils in the alabaster jars, and taste the loaded staleness of the air. Surry was drawn into a private world he never wanted to leave. That sight! That holy sight! A lifetime dream. The mesmerizing spell that gripped Surry was suddenly pierced when a hand seized his boot.

"My God, Surry, not a sound from you in almost two hours. What happened?" whispered Valerie, looking intently at her dazed husband crouched in front of her lantern.

Words seemed hopelessly inadequate when Surry attempted to answer. "Can't describe it. Take a look." He clumsily maneuvered himself backward, allowing Valerie to peer into the chiseled hole.

The light quivered in her hand as she pressed toward the tiny opening. Goosebumps formed on her arms and neck. While the slight flow of ancient air bathed her face, Valerie was transfixed by the awesome array. A profound silence overtook the pair as they sat stunned with astonishment.

"Surry, what is it?" The words escaped Valerie's parched

lips, breaking the delicious silence.

"I'm not sure," uttered Surry, "but it's magnificent!"

"Herihor?"

"Maybe," whispered Surry. "I can't make out the glyphs, but maybe the map is right."

Again Surry squinted at the dim arrangement of objects in the princely tomb. His gaze fell upon a distinct oval marking etched on the huge granite coffin. "It looks like a princely cartouche. If this is an unrecorded find, we're in for fireworks!"

"Let's get out of here so we can think straight," uttered Valerie quietly. "We'll tell the crew there's a cave-in. They won't go near it."

Surry gingerly pushed a pebble into the peephole. The dazed couple crawled back to the main passage, eager to get out to fresh air, sunlight and the reality of the day. After telling the crew of impending rockslides within, a danger sign was posted blocking the entrance to the tomb. Surry announced a closure to the worksite in order to request help for a "cave-in inspection."

To avoid being overheard, the Semaines ate lunch on the hotel's small patio. Surry stared blankly at the bougainvillea bushes which sheltered the table from the dusty road beyond. "We've got to level with the Antiquities Council, Val. This situation is too big for any shenanigans."

"What about Charles?"

"That ass will get his share in this thing after it's too late to come and loot the place for himself," Surry retorted.

"Calm down, Surry, we've got to think sensibly. What's first?"

"Number one, we go straight to the Chief of Antiquities and tell him we think we've found something. After he inspects the site, we'll call Blumfield. By that time, we can tell the Council that Charles is involved and maybe they'll reinstate his visa. After all, it *was* his map."

"Decent of you, Surry, but you're the one who had the resources to follow through. In the end it all belongs to the Egyptians anyway. For now, we call the shots."

"No need to get me any more hyped, Val, I'm edgy as hell now!" Surry ordered another beer.

CHAPTER 14

Luxor's Antiquities Director, Abdul Bassit, showed no emotion as he listened to Professor Semaine's report of his findings. The Arab man sat perfectly still except for the flutter of his turban's gauze under the overhead fan. His desk was in disarray with paper clutter, as was every other available tabletop piled with dusty notebooks, old photographs and unattended mail.

Bradford Dunn joined Surry and Valerie for the crucial meeting, while Roxy Morgan was left in charge of the locked worksite, making certain all was in order for the night guards to take over. Dunn listened intently to Surry's description of what had been viewed through the pierced hole in the limestone. Bradford, although being a quiet, conservative man, shivered with excitement in spite of the heat of the sun coming through the window.

The Director's words were tense. "This matter will be between us until more is known. You will take me to the tomb today. I must see for myself."

The Director moved decisively, instructing his assistant to take him in the official SUV to the West Valley. Bradford went ahead by ferry while Surry and Valerie sat quietly in the back seat of the Director's black vehicle which took the longer route crossing the new Nasser Bridge a few miles upriver from Luxor.

After being waved though the main gate leading to the Valley of the Kings, the vehicle reached the side road of the adjacent canyon. Entering the empty vastness of the West Valley burial grounds on a deserted July afternoon made one fully aware of the reference "valley of the dead." Nothing moved beyond the armed officers at the barricaded entrance. The security guards recognized Bassit's car and, after surveying the backseat passengers, waved them through. Not a tourist was in sight when the car turned onto the dusty road leading into the narrow gorge. The lookout sentries appeared as motionless specks above on the high cliffs. The desert below looked motionless in the still, hot air.

Bradford Dunn stood with Roxy near the opening of the tomb as the official's car approached in a swirl of dust. Dunn approached the vehicle, greeting the group as Bassit climbed out impatiently giving a terse order. "Unlock the entrance. I'm ready to go in."

Chief Bassit was a middle-aged man beginning to show the chunky roundness of bureaucratic comfort. Corpulence signaled the abundance of a successful life style in Egypt and was not looked upon with disfavor among the native population. The hefty director crawled awkwardly behind Surry along the tunnel's canvas covered ground toward the ghostly spectacle that lay before them.

Taking the small pebble from the chiseled hole at the end of the passage, Surry could not resist gazing once again at the sight beyond the barrier. He felt a nudge by the eager Egyptian who maneuvered himself into position in front of the tiny hole.

He let out a gasp as he pressed his eye to the rocky wall. "Praise Allah!" The startled man shed his stoic manner, repeating, "Praise is to Allah. Who knows of this?" he demanded.

"Only three of my team," responded Surry, as a fleeting mental image of Blumfield subdued his exuberance.

"No one can know of this until we have more knowledge. The Minister of Culture must be informed." Bassit continued to stare. The perspiration on the back of his neck glowed in the light of the lantern. "We go now. I must make decisions."

Taking another look at the precious sight before replacing the pebble, Surry beamed with satisfaction as he shuffled behind Bassit in the dark passage toward the pillared room of Amenhotep's tomb.

CHAPTER 15

Joan Kaufman's request for a second visit to Amenhotep's tomb received no response. Not a word. Finally, she had Fatime drive her to the West Valley on the pretense of visiting the restored tomb of King Ay located a few miles beyond Semaine's site. After a hurried tour of Ay's underground burial place, Joan directed her driver toward the dirt road leading to Amenhotep's tomb.

Inspector Rachid spotted the car, signaling it to stop as he rushed down the incline before the approaching vehicle came closer. Stillness hung over the area. Director Bassit's dark SUV was parked at the bottom of the slope and two armed guards stood alert beside the tomb's entrance.

"No visitors today," stated Rachid firmly to Joan's driver.

"I'm a personal friend of Doctor Semaine. Please let him know I am here," insisted Joan from the back seat.

"Impossible," retorted the inspector flatly. "The professor cannot be disturbed today. Perhaps another time."

Fatime sat stoically at the wheel surveying the scene, his discerning eye observing traces of fresh gravel on the nearby terrain. "Something different here," he muttered aloud, as he turned the car and headed out of the canyon with his silent passenger.

Joan did not stop to check her mail when she arrived at the Winter Palace, but went directly to her room to place a call to California.

"Something's happening at the site," Joan reported to Charles. "The thugs posted at the tomb entrance indicate a new level of security. They won't allow us near the place."

"Sound's interesting, most interesting. Good work, Joan." Charles sounded preoccupied. "Where's Fatime? I need to talk to him."

"He's in the bar downstairs. I'll get him. He can make the call from my room. I wish you were here."

"I just might be there, and soon. I'm beginning to wonder if the Professor is as honest as I thought." His voice trailed off in an unfriendly tone.

The bartender in the Victoria Bar handed Fatime the phone. "Get a pack of Marlboros and come up to my room," ordered Joan. "Mr. Blumfield wants to talk to you."

Fatime signed for the charges, adding a generous tip for the barman. He was pleased to work for Blumfield again after the long absence of his wealthy client. It was a relief to have well-paid employment during the hard times and he especially liked the duty of driving and watching out for Miss Kaufman. His hangout now was the best hotel in town. The confident-looking Egyptian sauntered out of the bar with two packs of cigarettes, one for Miss Kaufman and one for himself.

The luxurious old hotel was nearly vacant, except for the French tour groups, who tended to be fearless and could be counted on when the summer rates were favorable. The service staff was minimal; however, security crews were in full force hoping to display an atmosphere of safety for tourists who braved the alarming reports of bloodshed. The government posted additional guards at all visitor centers in an attempt to boost the sagging tourism trade.

Hotel personnel closely observed anyone entering the lobby, but Fatime's familiar face was welcome and his activities were unrestricted. His family was well-known and had been friendly with local merchants for decades. He climbed the thickly carpeted staircase to Joan's floor without interference.

Fatime's family home was a traditional mud-brick dwelling with canvas-covered windows on the West Bank of the Nile. The crowded multi-level living space belonged to his elderly parents who harbored the entire clan of Fatime's sisters and brothers, plus mates and children who were collected along the way. The structure was located on a breezy hillside and had a spacious inner courtyard for family activities.

The labyrinth of adobe buildings that Fatime shared with his parents had been haphazardly erected over an ancient workmen's cemetery dating from the pharaonic era. The backyard of the house led directly into a dome-like cave where the family kept a tangled menagerie of chickens, doves and rabbits. Beyond the nests, cages and beastly smells was a dirt passage leading downward into a maze of roughly hewed alcoves which contained mummified animals, small statuary, jewelry, decorated pots, and various other grave goods. The funerary objects that Fatime and his family marketed to tourists and collectors had augmented the family income for generations.

After the discovery of King Tutankhamen in the early twentieth century, Egyptian burial goods began to bring impressive prices from admirers around the globe causing government inspectors to heighten their patrol of the "workers hill." Officials rarely bothered to check beyond the farm animals and muggy barnyard odors that the hillside inhabitants encouraged in the caves on their property.

For decades, members of Fatime's family discreetly sold ancient pots, tools, beads and statues that came from the subterranean graves. Other items of more significant value, which members of the family pilfered while working with foreign archeological teams, were also hidden in the old underground caverns. For centuries, selling ancient tomb articles has supported scores of Arab families. To this day many citizens of Egypt consider marketing tomb artifacts a lucrative profession, even though officially illegal.

Although the government could not legitimately force out families who had homesteaded the gravesite hill hundreds of years ago, authorities were systematically buying what they could from private owners in the historic area. Most old Egyptians who had dealt in the sales of burial goods for a lifetime were far more interested in their clandestine source of revenue than they were in moving and starting anew. Change is not welcome under the Sahara sun and tradition is not easily dislodged. To the majority of the natives in the small town of Luxor, progress is not a priority.

Fatime was taller than most of his countrymen, well-fed and solid. He did not have the distinctive African features often found in Upper Egypt. Except for his white turban and gray *jelabiya*, he could easily pass for a handsome Greek or Italian citizen.

"Is Miss Kaufman in the room?" Charles asked from San Francisco. "I don't want her involved in this conversation, Fatime."

"I understand your message, sir. She is in her bedroom."

"I want to come to Egypt soon, very soon. I'll need papers to enter the country. Get me the surveyor's passport.

You've seen him; Dunn is Semaine's right hand man and he's about my age and build. Wait for him to go out alone and do what you have to. Make it clean and permanent in a place where he won't need ID papers. Can you handle that?" questioned Charles in a low menacing voice. "If all goes smoothly, send me his passport and ID by overnight express. You will be well paid."

"I can do what you say, sir." Fatime displayed a confident smile as he watched Joan Kaufman enter the sitting room. She smelled of lavender, and her flowing *jelabiya* looked fresh and cool.

"Did you straighten the salary thing out with Mr. Blumfield?" she asked as Fatime hung up the phone.

"All is good. He is fair with me and my family. No problem."

"Glad to hear that, Fatime. Shall we let him buy us dinner tonight? I don't want to eat alone."

He was particularly handsome when he smiled. "With pleasure, Madame."

CHAPTER 16

The gossip network among the Arab community was surprisingly efficient. Taxi drivers, hotel employees, tomb workers and shop owners had ample time to exchange stories during their frequent cigarette breaks. Few villagers could afford television or bothered to buy a newspaper; they much preferred exchanging local news among themselves in huddles along the Nile.

The desk clerk at the Nefertari Hotel alerted Fatime when a request came from Bradford Dunn to schedule a driver for an all-day journey. Fatime's brother-in-law, Kom, dutifully waited with his cab in front of the hotel at six o'clock on Saturday morning.

Bradford Dunn had resolved to revisit the sacred bull cemetery, where Surry had taken him a year ago. The unusual site and bizarre legends of pharaonic bull worship had fascinated him and he felt certain that *Archaeology Magazine* would be interested in an article about the unique royal bull rituals.

Ancient Egyptians believed that gods inhabited the bodies of certain animals and the Apis Bull cult was among the most highly revered of animal deities. The ruling pharaohs of the Middle Kingdom from 2000 B.C. kept prize bulls on the palace grounds, designating one favorite bull as leader and most honored of the group. It was believed that the "god of strength and endurance" inhabited the chief bull during its lifetime and when that bull died the spirit would move into another living bull's body. Upon death, the honored bull's body received sacred mummification and burial ceremonies, and then the hunt was on for the new "leader of the sacred bulls." Supposedly the symbol of authenticity for choosing the new leader of the bulls was the rare mark of a black circle on the tongue of a young calf. Such a calf would be singled out and examined and then trained as the new Chief Apis Bull of the ruling pharaoh's compound.

Bradford awakened early that Saturday morning and was dressed and ready long before the taxi arrived. The lean 67-year-old surveyor was well prepared for his outing in the desert; his backpack was neatly arranged with notebooks, camera, film, water and sunscreen, plus passport and permits for checkpoints along the way.

While the eager adventurer was having coffee and biscuits alone in the hotel breakfast room, the cook appeared with a sack of sandwiches he had requested for the long day ahead. Slipping the lunch carefully into the backpack, Bradford went to the street and was pleased to find the taxi waiting. The driver was on time, which was not always the case in the slow rhythm of the Sahara Desert. Bradford greeted the driver with instructions for the day's itinerary. Kom answered in spotty English, indicating he was vaguely familiar with the bull's obscure burial site and estimated the ride would take about two hours.

"Let's get started," responded Bradford, flush with

anticipation. The early desert air was pleasant, yet one could sense the quiet invasion of heat as the eastern sky became fiery over the mountain peaks. Near the edge of the town, worn-out horses, not yet hooked up to buggies, were munching the morning feedbag feast before beginning the monotonous daily passenger routine.

After two check points and several detours on dusty roads, Kom stopped to ask directions of a young donkey rider along the roadside. The bronzed youth with black, curly hair willingly pointed toward the low hills rising to the west. Seeing an automobile in the bleak desert was an uncommon sight for the boy and at first he gallantly refused the money Bradford offered him. He proudly rode on after taking the dollar bill, turning back to smile broadly, as if to say, "See, I am rich. I have a donkey."

The shock absorbers in the vintage Peugeot needed serious repair, especially apparent when the rough dirt road became raw desert, but Bradford jolted along in a state of gleeful optimism. The car bumped cautiously along the flattest paths of the cracked desert clay until Kom brought the over-heated vehicle to a halt within walking distance of the low earthen mounds ahead.

Kom opened the door for his passenger, motioning toward the mysterious mounds on the horizon. Leaning on the hood of his car, Kom lit a cigarette and calmly observed Bradford stride toward the historic ruins. Other than the two human intruders, not a sign of life stirred in the solemn surroundings. Only feeble dry weeds clung to the scorched desert.

The abandoned bull cemetery was not a site sought out by casual tourists. There were no road signs pointing to the abandoned animal shrines and, unless one knew the history of the sacred beasts, visiting the ruins of the once magnificent setting would be meaningless. In recent times local natives from the nearest villages used the gully as a landfill for garbage. The ravine, punctured with caves, had been looted by scavengers throughout the ages and, except for several faded decorations, they currently resembled crude hideouts for nomads.

Bradford glanced in the direction of the Nile, unable to detect any sign of the palm trees that lined the distant river. It was a serene and lonely place. After trudging several minutes in the hot morning sun, Bradford reached the top of a mound and reached for a water bottle in his backpack.

His gaze was transfixed on the cave openings below. Not even a wisp of breeze disturbed the stillness of the macabre caverns before him. An occasional hawk flew overhead searching for prey that had died in the desert, but it seemed even insects had abandoned the sterile setting. The overwhelming silence enveloped Bradford in a trance, as if he were the only person to discover the eerie setting.

After a couple of hours exploring and photographing the strangely shaped openings, Bradford rested on a flat boulder to eat his lunch. As he inspected his film supply while observing the pale hieroglyphs on fallen stones nearby, he was startled by a rustle behind him.

The surveyor's last living thought was that a snake was in this barren spot. A moment later his crushed skull no longer registered thoughts of any kind.

Fatime's brother-in-law quickly rifled through the dead man's belongings and reached for the passport pouch. His hand stroked the expensive camera and the surveyor's sleek steel pen. Disregarding instructions to take nothing except the man's ID papers, Kom could not resist the impressive camera and pen, quickly pushing the items into his shoulder bag. He wrapped Bradford's limp body in a coarse camel blanket and took the man for a final journey far into the desert.

Back at Amenhotep's tomb, work schedules were halted. The Egyptian crew had been given the week off with pay, with the excuse that cave-in conditions called for thorough safety measures. Risky work conditions were commonplace in tombs and the advance pay envelopes squelched any probing questions from the work team.

On Saturday morning, Surry and Val went to the West Valley tomb with Director Bassit's assistants to prepare the crawlspace for officials from Cairo. The Director had alerted the Minister of Culture of the developing event and recommended that the Minister observe the situation with his own eyes as soon as it was safe to do so.

Armed guards were on twenty-four-hour watch at the tomb entrance, allowing only Chief Bassit, the Semaines, and Rachid clearance to enter. Bassit ordered activity in the vicinity to be kept at a minimum to avoid unwanted attention before the Minister of Culture and experts from Cairo could schedule an inspection of the discovery.

Surry spent most of the weekend with Rachid sealing cracks in the tunnel and laying reed mats over the uneven canvas covering on the floor of the passageway for easier access in the future. Each time Surry approached the end of the passage he removed the stone from the hole and gazed again at the stockpile on the other side of the wall. He needed constant assurance that it was not a dream.

By Sunday afternoon, the Semaines' emotions were in high gear as they readied for the arrival of prominent visitors. Late Sunday afternoon they reluctantly left the locked tomb in the care of guards and caught the ferry to the East Bank. Surry left messages in the mailboxes of Bradford and Roxy requesting a dinner meeting for eight o'clock at the Mercure Hotel.

The Mercure's second floor restaurant was decorated with a sorry mix of 1970's modern furniture. The garish floral upholstery on the sturdy wooden chairs blended restlessly with a swirling rug pattern. Several potted palms somewhat calmed the surroundings, but it was the grand panorama of the Nile from the oversized windows that salvaged the lackluster atmosphere.

By eight-thirty, Valerie, Roxy and Surry had finished a round of drinks. "It's not like Bradford to be late. Do you think he missed the message?" The professor looked intently across the empty tables toward the greeter standing at the door.

"Hope he's not sick. I haven't seen him since Friday. He was excited about going to the bull cemetery on Saturday," added Roxy hesitantly.

"Guess we'd better check. I'll call his room," Surry said, pushing his chair back and pulling out his cell phone.

Surry returned to the table looking puzzled. "Strange. The desk clerk said that no one has seen Brad since breakfast on Saturday. No answer in his room either."

"I hope nothing's wrong," Valerie said calmly. "So much going on lately, it's hard to keep up."

"You two go ahead and order while I make a quick trip to the hotel. No sense going over plans until Brad is with us." Surry said absently. The excitement of the new find was dampened by Surry's concern.

A wave of foreboding rippled through Surry as he approached the Nefertari Hotel's reception desk. Ordinarily Dunn was precise and punctual; an unannounced absence was unlike him. Surry's mind raced as he reminisced that he often neglected to compliment his trusted associate, always assuming that Brad knew his expertise was appreciated. The surveyor was reserved, almost shy, carrying out duties with quiet efficiency. Always ready with appropriate instruments to fit every situation, the loyal co-worker had the ideal qualifications for Surry's needs in the ghostly tombs.

At the reception desk, Amed willingly handed Surry the key to Bradford's room while encouraging the professor not to worry about his friend. The kind Arab seemed confident that Mr. Dunn had taken a weekend journey and would return soon.

Bradford's room was in neat order, typical of the occupant's meticulous habits. Camera gone, backpack gone; all the usual articles taken for a foray in the desert. Surry felt better, recalling Bradford's eagerness to visit the bull pits. Had he planned to stay the entire weekend?

Surry locked the room and hurried back to the reception desk. "Amed, see if you can find the driver that Mr. Dunn hired on Saturday morning. Maybe he knows something. I'll check with you after dinner."

Sleeping was troubled for the Semaines that night. The impending arrival of the Minister of Culture was concern enough…and now Dunn's puzzling absence. At four in the morning, Surry kicked off the sheets and headed for the shower.

"Hell with it. I can't sleep," he growled when he saw Valerie stretching. "Sorry to wake you."

"You didn't. Can't sleep either," she yawned.

"I'll check if Brad's back yet." Surry pulled on his pants and tee shirt, pushing his bare feet into shoes. It was one of those mornings he did not need caffeine for a jump-start.

Surry returned visibly distressed. "Not there. Something's wrong. Brad wouldn't miss work on a Monday morning. Let's hope he shows up today with a good explanation. I'll ask Roxy to stay at the hotel to check with the cab driver when Amed finds him. We have to meet Chief Bassit at the site. It's too late now to cancel the morning meeting."

"So much for the summer schedule," Valerie's voice wavered. Bradford's disappearance, the officials coming from Cairo, plus the looming necessity of informing Blumfield about the found vault, overshadowed the thrill of the mysterious stash waiting in the West Valley.

"You know, Val, uncovering an important find like this has been a hope of mine for decades. We should be popping champagne corks by now. Real life is a lot different than the dream, isn't it?"

Their admired colleague, Bradford Dunn, was not going to return. His body was slowly baking in a sandy grave in the distant desert. His passport was in the hands of Charles Blumfield, whose new glasses and groomed beard bore an uncanny resemblance to Brad's passport photo.

CHAPTER 17

Charles Blumfield left San Francisco soon after receiving the Air Express package containing the dead man's passport and identification papers. His trimmed beard, wire-framed glasses and canvas hat allowed Charles to pass through Cairo customs without incident with Bradford's passport. His entrance was eased by the impressive archaeological permit from Egypt's Ministry of Culture.

The curb outside the Cairo airport was lined with taxis and private cars. Charles selected a stout, neatly dressed driver standing beside a blue BMW sedan and he proceeded to negotiate terms for the 400-mile drive to Luxor. With bottled water and a sack lunch in his backpack, Blumfield braced himself for the sweltering desert journey to Luxor. The air conditioning in the recent model car helped compensate for the 115-degree heat. The jet-lagged passenger lapsed into a fitful sleep in the clammy air of the backseat.

Skillfully navigating Egyptian roads, the Arab driver dodged wandering livestock, donkey carts, tour buses, and roaming bands of natives. It was evening by the time

Charles was delivered to the entrance of the Winter Palace Hotel where Joan was anxiously waiting.

Miss Kaufman was a familiar guest in good standing and her gentleman caller raised no eyebrows among the hotel staff. The couple headed straight to Joan's suite where Charles pushed his suitcase into a corner, took off his shirt and shoes and gladly accepted a cold beer while stretching out on the queen-size bed. He had not finished his beer before drifting off to sleep in rumpled slacks.

In the morning Joan thoughtfully studied Charles across the linen-covered breakfast cart laden with platters of fruit, croissants and coffee. With a pensive smile, she recalled the many breakfasts she had shared with this man. Though he had aged, an appealing masculinity still lingered in his well-cared-for body.

"You look good, Joan. I often think of our good times together."

"We have some history, don't we? I've grown up a bit. I'm less idealistic and probably better company now." She smiled when his hand pulled her toward him.

When his lips touched hers, past currents flowed again. It wasn't poetic love, but they understood each other's passions well enough to generate a heated reunion. Joan did not resist when Charles adeptly unbuttoned her silk pajama top, sliding his palms across her breasts to her bare back, pressing his body to hers. Joan had distanced herself from relationships for the past couple of years and her senses were over-ripe. The span of years since their last affair dissolved into a flurry of revived passion.

An unusual enchantment drifts over the Sahara dunes, an exotic trancelike attitude that sensitive souls find hard to describe and even more difficult to resist. The same hypnotic spell that came over Charles and Joan had almost allowed Joan to succumb to Fatime's gruff advances only a week ago.

The pair galloped with delirium and exploded into a frothy jolt that unleashed the tensions of mind and muscles. Glistening with perspiration, Charles parted from Joan's damp body and fell limply beside her, savoring the contented silence. The fiery encounter melted away the years since their awkward parting in San Francisco. They could talk freely again, their grudges and rusty hostilities blown away.

After a refreshing nap, Charles relaxed with lunch on the terrace overlooking the Nile. He stared contently at the billowing linen sails of the feluccas floating lazily up the river. The simple handcrafted boats were now used mostly for tourists. Their construction had changed little during the centuries when the small wooden vessels were a vital means of transportation for passengers and commerce.

Charles did not want to take the chance of being recognized and was determined to avoid the busy streets of Luxor during daylight hours. Joan and Fatime managed to keep up with current rumors during their regular daily errands, while Charles planned furtive forays under the cover of night.

CHAPTER 18

Clusters of white turbans appeared on every corner of Luxor's public areas no matter what the season. Gossip was a favorite pastime among the men hovering around the cabs and horse drawn carriages. Especially interesting was the latest scuttlebutt concerning a missing American archaeologist. The Arabs joked and took bets on the chances for a foreigner to survive if lost among the rolling desert dunes.

Occasionally tourists lose their way or meet an unhappy ending in the vast Saharan desert, but usually it is a case of a naïve solo traveler on limited funds or one who takes foolhardy risks. Foreign women are advised not to venture in the North African Desert unaccompanied under any circumstances. Bradford Dunn should have heeded this advice also.

Ancient desert dwellers have their own basic code of ethics, which is based on helping each other endure the hardships of life in this arid land. As in most cultures, if it means selling information or artifacts or doing dastardly deeds to feed the clan, so be it. Loyalty among old traditional families was tough to deter, either by their nation's legal system or by interfering foreigners.

Motives for dealing in unlawful services and contraband among the local tribes were not driven by greed so much as the effort to maintain a family's pride and welfare. Typical west bank dwellings had basic dirt floors; however, each Friday a plentiful family dinner was expected for family members. Providing a television set for the matriarch was a luxury that the woman put to constant use while watching over a brood of grandchildren when other members of the group were off at work.

The daily customs of villagers didn't necessarily translate to Western ideals for the good life or the pursuit of happiness, but their own clannish codes made perfect sense to men like Fatime and his friends. They were content and at peace with Allah, who guided them to various paths of survival and fulfillment.

What motives Charles Blumfield had were of little interest to Fatime and Kom as long as cash was paid for services rendered. Fatime's relationship with Blumfield functioned on a simple premise: a good source of American dollars kept his Egyptian family independent from moneylenders. Life was cheap in this ancient land and it was of minor concern to Fatime if some people had to die prematurely to maintain the existence of his relatives.

Cousins, uncles, aunts, brothers, sisters, in-laws and neighbors were closely intertwined in local villages. The fraternal band of Egyptians on the hillside near the West Bank ferry dock considered the adobe homes as well as the adjacent noble cemetery to be their rightful property, bound by their own rules of protection. Tourists and outsiders were viewed by some as an annoying invasion, only tolerated to provide a source of income for communal interests.

Director Bassit shared the view of many of his fellow citizens and had little affection for bothersome foreigners. Underneath all Bassit's verbosity about fairness and objectivity, he basically considered Westerners to be longtime plunderers of Egypt's magnificent heritage. Archaeologists from distant countries were endured because they arrived with money, talent and jobs for the locals, but beneath Bassit's tough, tanned skin he snickered at the mores of the Western World. Far too many of Egypt's brilliant treasures were locked up in foreign museums or on display in distant public parks and squares. The time had come for outsiders to stop stealing the glories of Egypt's past.

Local vendors, guides and carriage drivers thrived on rumors and tales of scandal to gossip about during street corner gatherings. The missing American archaeologist was a tasty topic, and then there was also a rumor that riches had been found in a nearby tomb. Bassit had been making numerous trips to the desolate West Valley recently, raising the curiosity of guards along the route.

Bassit had not pressed the Ministry in Cairo of the urgency in regard to the visit to the West Valley site as he had assured Doctor Semaine. If what was uncovered turned out to be the lost Herihor burial place, it was too significant for Americans to claim credit. Bassit wanted to be sure such a major find would be credited to himself and that meant quick work before elaborate details were relayed to Cairo.

First, the cache of riches had to be identified further and then an outside entrance to the lost tomb needed to be located. Other than the Semaines and Director Bassit, no one had seen the dazzling spectacle through the hole pierced in the rocky wall. The regular work team continued to be on paid leave due to the so-called "unsafe work conditions." Although recent activity had caused gossip among the natives, details were sketchy and tales of treasure were commonplace in the ancient town.

In preparation for the inspection by the Minister of Culture, which Bassit was in charge of scheduling, Semaine and the Director worked feverishly, chipping a crawlspace through the wall at the end of the hidden passageway. It was a sweaty process; however, the work could not be trusted to anyone else.

When the jagged opening became large enough to squeeze through, Bassit insisted on being first and pushed his bulky body into the ghostly chamber. Surry quickly followed and the men found themselves in a cavern with silent spirits which had not been disturbed for centuries.

"Dear God!" gasped Surry as he stretched to a standing position pointing his lantern around the hallowed shrine.

"Miracle from Allah," breathed Bassit, mesmerized by the hoard of artifacts surrounding the two stunned men.

Radiant gold stars painted on the blue domed ceiling glowed with uncanny brightness in the light of Bassit's lantern. A fine layer of silky dust coated the disheveled linen shroud partially covering the massive granite sarcophagus. The slight disorder among the stacks of artifacts indicated an invasion in earlier times.

Surry and Bassit stood spellbound, resisting the urge to reach out and touch the relics around them. Gilded wooden cots, mahogany chairs, carved stools, chests inlaid with ivory and neatly tied-up reed boxes lined the chamber walls. It was all too delicate, too ancient, and too precious to take the chance of hastily disturbing objects that might crumble from shock after centuries of peaceful darkness.

A superbly painted bentwood chariot with two spare

wheels and a hardened leather harness rested against a far wall near a sealed, heavy wooden door. Bassit and Surry glared at each other; no words were spoken. The sight shook their souls and silenced their voices. For men who had rummaged around antiquities most of their adult lives, they were as unprepared as schoolboys for what surrounded them. They considered themselves to be rational men, yet standing in the hidden treasure-filled sanctuary they felt as if they were in the grip of ghostly spirits.

The professor recognized gold statuary, silver shields, swords, gilded masks and cartouches dating from prior regimes. Herihor! It must be Herihor! Artifacts, evidently from other dynasties, added evidence that this was the long lost Pharaoh known to plunder royal tombs for precious loot, adding to the wealth of his own stockpile of riches. Plagued by an era of rampant grave robbing, Herihor had commanded his priests to gather gold and silver from various shrines of other rulers in order to preserve them for what he called "safety reasons" in the underground sanctuary being built for his own "afterlife."

Whether motivated by greed or a sincere interest in conservation of sacred objects, Herihor managed to amass one of the most bountiful hoards of treasure in the documented history of Egyptian kings. Dynastic scrolls describe Herihor's life of splendor, lavishing gold gifts on his favorite wives, concubines, priests and generals while never depleting his reserves of precious inventory. Herihor did not inherit the throne as a direct descendant of the royal family, but accomplished his climb to power by his wary manipulations as a high priest. He ruled only a few years in the eleventh century B.C.; however, during his reign he had command over all the temples and tombs of Upper Egypt and could distribute confiscated sacred items of preceding rulers as he saw fit.

Professor Semaine and Director Bassit sensed that the extraordinary chamber where they were standing matched evidence linked to the lost twenty-first dynasty pharaoh. Barely able to steady his hand, the professor pulled out his cell phone and took several quick photos while Bassit's back was turned.

"Very important to find the outside entrance to this tomb," whispered the Inspector. "This news cannot be revealed until we locate the original entry in the cliff. Cairo officials cannot come until there is a better entrance for distinguished government men. They would not be pleased to use the small tunnel."

"I understand," agreed Surry, excitedly. "I can return tomorrow with proper equipment to prepare for them."

"No. Your permit does not include this project. I will arrange everything!" stated Bassit abruptly.

Surry's heart sank. He was in a foreign land with little power to make demands. His dream was slipping away. "I will assist you," Surry added solemnly. He would not be pushed aside so easily.

CHAPTER 19

Acutely aware of his own deceit, Charles Blumfield did not put trust in others. He was not satisfied with the sketchy reports that Surry had relayed to him by phone. Joan's description of activities in the West Valley was far more tantalizing. Charles was determined to see for himself what was taking place in the tomb of Amenhotep III and he instructed Fatime to arrange a clandestine visit.

The two night guards at the West Valley tomb were local natives known to Fatime. Persuaded by a generous bribe, the guards were willing to allow two curious American tourists to enter Tomb WV22 for a moonlight adventure. No harm done if Fatime guaranteed that nothing would be disturbed or taken. Fatime organized the pick-up at the Winter Palace Hotel for Friday at midnight.

Blumfield's restlessness was soothed by making love in a cool, dim hotel room while outside the midday sun baked Luxor's asphalt streets. Hiding out in an attractive woman's suite at the luxurious hotel suited his idea of intrigue. He wallowed in the juicy delights of sex and thoughts of adventure while passing the afternoon until crossing the

Nile at midnight. Joan accepted Charles Blumfield for the dashing rogue he was. She was more mature now, having learned to enjoy the moment at hand without asking too many questions or making demands for the future.

Charles had the reputation among his friends and colleagues of satisfying his own needs first and foremost. His wife, Flora, knew his habits better than anyone. She asked few favors of her husband other than the appearance of a successful lifestyle in California society. The Blumfields had agreed to a marriage of convenience while each pursued individual interests.

There were sufficient communal assets to bond the marriage even though romance and sentiment had faded long ago. Their daughter and son were launched in their own careers and the lavish Cathedral Hill apartment was spacious enough to provide Charles and Flora with separate living quarters—a civilized arrangement that worked socially and financially. Flora occupied her energies with fundraising for the San Francisco Ballet while Charles went freely about acting the hero in his own private movie. Romping in the Middle East with a pretty lady surrounded by sacred temples and ancient tombs was a role he relished.

Joan had learned to live with compromises. Cavorting with the wealthy playboy was more appealing than her day job of satisfying requests from Hollywood starlets for constant publicity. Currently Charles was paying the bills, plus the bonus of a pleasing frolic in bed. He was a good lover. Perhaps Joan would not have felt so smug about her circumstances if she knew that her playmate was capable of murder. She was not aware of Bradford Dunn's passport which Charles had in his possession.

Dressed in khaki garb with brimmed hats, Charles and Joan looked the part of typical tourists as they greeted

Fatime in front of the Winter Palace at the appointed hour. The midnight summer air was cool and welcoming after the day's intense temperatures. A slight breeze from the Nile felt like silk flowing over Joan's skin.

The tree-lined promenade along the river still churned with families socializing in the coolness of the night. Local inhabitants hibernated during the stifling afternoons, dining late in their adobe homes before congregating for gossip along the Nile. Small children hovered near the segregated groups of black-veiled women while, close by, clouds of cigarette smoke encircled the clusters of men.

Fatime's Mercedes passed only a few cars during the drive south on the new highway toward the modern Nasser Bridge. The couple in the backseat was equipped with ordinary sightseeing gear: bottles of water, cameras and an ample supply of twenty-dollar bills. Their quest, however, was anything but ordinary.

Among the locals, Fatime was a familiar face and he was usually waived through roadway checkpoints without an inspection. Terrorism activities had subsided somewhat under the country's military takeover and the night-duty guards welcomed the green bills as they raised the barriers for Fatime and his passengers. The Mercedes was the lone car on the dark, deserted road that led toward the Royal Acropolis.

The only other activities in the vicinity at that time of night were night watchmen changing shifts and two sentries on duty at the deserted gate to the Valley of the Kings. As the guards eyed the visitors with suspicion, Fatime flashed a broad white smile at the uniformed man holding a M-22 rifle. Luckily, the man recognized the driver.

"My passengers are here to write an article for the American *Traveler* magazine. They want to photograph with no tourists around. Their magazine will pay extra for a night permit," stated Fatime while shaking hands with the guard and leaving five bills in the man's hand.

With no perceptible acknowledgement of the bills, the official looked into the backseat and studied the faces of the occupants. "Step out of the car," he ordered.

"They going to scan the photography equipment, that's all," Fatime interjected, noting Blumfield's discomfort.

Both Joan and Charles climbed out of the backseat and stood silently while the guards checked their clothing and cameras with a metal detector. Fatime opened the trunk for inspection. "All clear. Two hours only. Next time…a valid permit."

"*Shukran*," Fatime said rolling up the car window and accelerating slowly.

Blumfield leaned back with a satisfied grin. He reached for Joan's hand, placing it on the mound rising between his legs. "You're good, Fatime. You'll be paid well. Step on it; two hours isn't much time."

"No worry, Mr. B, two hours means three or four in Egypt time." He drove faster than usual as he turned onto the bumpy dirt road leading into the starlit West Valley burial grounds. This checkpoint was not guarded, as traffic was at a standstill during the night.

No movement could be seen except Fatime's headlights bouncing eerie shadows on the jagged ridges of the gorge. The aura of solitude within the confines of the dark cliffs gave the appearance of an uninhabited planet—a perfect hangout for souls of the dead. Charles and Joan rode in the quiet of a peculiar void that was rarely found in their hectic modern lifestyle and a true picture of the Bedouin word *sahara*—nothingness.

The tires crunched to a halt just below the entrance of

Tomb WV22. A wall of stillness dropped around the passengers after the last whine of the engine. A bulky figure came out of the dimness toward the car.

"*Salaam*," grunted the security guard. "The patrol gate called. This is not usual. It is a special privilege that we give to you. No one can know. Do you understand? I must look at what you bring with you, then two hours for photos and touch nothing."

"You are a friend, Mohammed," said Fatime softy, slipping the burly watchman several bills while shaking hands.

The guard's fingers probed the cameras and shoulder bags. Joan bristled at the closeness of the leathery hands as the man stared at her with narrowed eyes. "Follow Fatime...and mind the steps. There must be no accidents."

Joan could feel the tremor of Blumfield's arm as he pulled her up the rocky incline toward the unlocked gate leading into an opening in the cliff. "I've waited a long time for this, Joan."

The darkness of the tomb was profound with only the halogen flashlights slicing through the blackness. Descending steeply on the pharaoh's funerary route, the crumbling wall sketches along the way seemed to move with the dancing beams of the light. The smell, while not unpleasant, was curiously musty and stale, filling the air with a mood of reverence which discouraged idle conversation. Fatime, Charles and Joan carefully made their way down the second set of steps and across the wooden planks that covered the forbidding deep well shaft which was meant to discourage intruders. Muffled echoes from the hollow below returned their footsteps as they crossed the narrow overpass.

Blumfield suddenly dropped Joan's hand as they entered

the first pillared chamber. His flashlight followed the dusty walls until it illuminated the rough boards braced with stones on the south side. He felt instinctively that beyond that haphazard pile of stones was what he had crossed the ocean to see.

Charles and Fatime pushed away the rocks, loosening the wooden board that covered the crawlspace. "I'm going in there," Charles whispered excitedly. "I'll call you two if I need help."

"I'm going, too," stated Joan emphatically, not wanting to be left in the dark with Fatime.

"It's cramped, Joan, and I don't know what's in there."

"I'm right behind you," Joan struggled to steady her voice. The urge to follow Charles was stronger than her actual courage.

Charles was a big man and his frame left little room for maneuvering along the dark cavity. The unknown, the stillness, and the blackness made every inch forward a challenge of determination. Charles liked daring acts, but this dark journey in an ancient burial ground surpassed his cravings. Joan crawled along nervously in the dust, pondering what had driven her to this bizarre folly.

Breathing in the stuffy passageway was not easy and their heartbeats quickened. In spite of the midnight air outside, both Charles and Joan were damp with perspiration. For the first time in Joan's life she understood the power of claustrophobia. She felt panicky with an urge to turn back. Blumfield's sudden stop in front jerked her out of a woozy stupor.

"Just ahead…. I see boards. You all right?" Charles struggled awkwardly to glance back at Joan.

"Not great, but I'll make it."

Charles pulled closer to the board at the end of the

tunnel. As he let it fall to the ground, he lifted his beam in the direction of the hollowness beyond. Silently he stared at the mysterious scene taking shape.

"Good God! The bastard was lying!" The words flowed automatically as he glared into the ghostly chamber.

Joan squeezed close to Charles. "What's there?"

"We're going to find out. Come on."

Charles squeezed through the opening with Joan clutching the back of his jacket. Time and place lost meaning as they gazed wide-eyed around the sacred burial chamber.

Charles breathed a low whistle. "Pay dirt! That little prick professor is going to find out who he's dealing with."

Joan didn't move or speak. Her stunned expression was of disbelief.

"Rich pharaoh, for sure," mumbled Charles, his face flushed. "Check the size of that sarcophagus. This could be it!"

Charles moved automatically to a slender wooden statue, about eight inches tall, perched on a stack of linen-wrapped boxes. The exquisitely-carved rosewood image wore a jeweled neckpiece and wrists adorned with finely-wrought gold cuffs. Except for a faint layer of dust, the polychrome figure with glaring ivory eyes looked brightly painted.

Charles gingerly reached for the object. "This goes with me, for proof. My map brought Semaine here and I'll see that I get the fucking credit!"

He stepped toward the huge pink granite sarcophagus and ran his fingers over the etched hieroglyphs. He quickly snapped two photos. "The lid has been disturbed, but most of it looks intact. I've seen all I need to for now. Let's get back before the guards get jumpy."

Almost mechanically, Joan's fingers wrapped around a

small jasper replica of Anubis, the guardian dog of the dead. Hypnotized by the piercing ruby eyes, Joan murmured, "I'll never forget this night. Anubis will be my touchstone."

"Shove it inside your blouse. I have the rosewood lady tucked in my jacket. We're out of here!"

Still mesmerized by the exotic sight, Joan and Charles were propelled through the narrow tunnel in a daze. Fatime was smoking while crouched against the wall of the pillared room.

"Did you see something?"

Charles was guarded. He trusted Fatime to a point, but not enough to relay what he had just experienced.

"We saw some relics, but must wait to see if they're important. It's time to go."

Fatime led the way up the incline of the dark passage. Their exhilaration was veiled by the cloak of night. Fatime shook hands with the guards, again folding a bill in each of their eager palms. The watchmen were somber. "No one can know about this. You may not visit again without a permit."

The ride to the Winter Palace in the hush of early morning was unusually quiet. Joan's thoughts floated in the world of the dead. The fever of discovery pounded in the veins of Blumfield. Visions of fame heated his brain.

Serenity hung over the banks of the Nile in a fragrant morning mist when Fatime pulled the Mercedes into the circular driveway of the hotel. His passengers stopped at the hotel's entrance to glance at the vapor rising from the river which appeared like a hazy sketch on parchment. Beneath the couple's calm appearance their senses were turbulent. When the door of the suite slammed shut, the flood of energy culminated in a big bang of lust. It was a night they would remember.

Early the next morning, Fatime picked up Charles for the journey to the Cairo airport. Twenty-four hours later, the American passed unquestioned through Egyptian customs using Bradford Dunn's passport. He handed the customs officials forged retail receipts for the nice little "reproductions" of an Egyptian goddess and a royal dog.

Arriving at the Paris-Orly Airport, Dunn's passport served its last purpose. The dead man's stolen papers were burned to ashes after Charles locked the door of his room in the city's posh Hôtel de Crillon. He had used his own perfectly valid passport at the reception desk. There would be no record that a man named Charles Blumfield had entered or left Egypt during the past three years.

CHAPTER 20

Roxy Morgan was frantic. No one had heard from Bradford Dunn for two weeks. Egyptian authorities were slow to respond to reports of missing American tourists, as foreign visitors were known for failing to communicate while on desert escapades. The Luxor police had made routine inquires, but without the urgency that obsessed Bradford's colleagues. Surry Semaine's nerves were edgy on several fronts and he finally began sounding the alarm with an insistent call to the United States Embassy in Cairo.

The cab driver who had picked up Bradford had come forward on his own accord when he heard that he was needed for questioning. He stated that his passenger requested a ride to the sacred bull pits early one Saturday morning. Upon arrival at the pits, the American photographer unloaded his equipment and supplies and asked to left alone to do his work. Bradford paid the driver for the entire day, with instructions to be picked up at five that afternoon.

Kom insisted that he dutifully returned to the pits at five o'clock, but was unable to find Mr. Dunn. He walked the area but finally decided that his passenger had met friends or had hiked alone to the next village. After waiting at the site for an hour, Kom drove his cab back to town without giving the incident much more thought. He had long ago given up trying to figure out the strange habits of Westerners.

Luxor authorities performed a routine inspection of Kom's taxi, which resembled any other overused Egyptian vehicle. It revealed nothing out of the ordinary about the taxi or Kom's story. They made a basic search of the grounds of the bull pits, which offered neither distinguishable tire tracks nor footprints after being exposed to the hot desert winds. There was no indication of foul play on the premises. On rare occasions the strange caves had a few curious visitors, but most of the time the grounds were deserted and ignored by the tourist office. No witnesses came forth to dispute Kom's statement and he was not detained by police.

When Bradford's younger brother, Eric, was notified in Denver, he immediately boarded a plane to Egypt to look into the matter personally. Their eighty-seven-year-old widowed mother was not yet informed that her son was missing.

Surry and Valerie carried on the best they could with the exploration of the new discovery while Roxy was to oversee the reports about Bradford. While waiting for Eric Dunn's arrival from Colorado, Roxy stubbornly retraced her partner's steps before the fateful day when he was last seen. She hired Kom to go back over the route that had been taken when he drove Bradford to the burial grounds.

Kom was not overly concerned by the curiosity of the young American girl; in fact, he was happy to have a good fare for the day. After he had passed the scrutiny of the

Luxor officers, the lady from America posed no threat. On the contrary, a full-bodied blonde passenger was especially welcomed by the bearded taxi driver.

Roxy Morgan was not at ease sitting in the same back seat that had transported Brad. A sense of gloom hovered over her as she rode along imbued with feelings of Bradford's presence. She stared thoughtfully at the tanned neck of the driver in front and caught his dark eyes observing her in the rear-view mirror. Even though Roxy possessed a robust sense of courage, it occurred to her that this ride should have waited until someone from the team took the journey with her.

Roxy broke the silence. "Did Mr. Dunn say that he was meeting someone at the bull pits?"

"Nothing about other people. Just to take pictures alone. He did not want me to stay. I returned as he ordered, but did not find him. It is his business if he leaves before I come back."

"Do you know that he is still missing?"

"My brother said police wanted information from me. At once I went to them. They could see it is not my problem. I was paid to drive and that is what I did."

"We fear for his life. It is serious."

"This is a big desert. I think he is seeing other places and he will be back soon."

"It is not the way of my friend to make us worry." Roxy's voice softened as Kom turned off the dirt road toward the bull cemetery. She realized she was nervously chattering too much. It was a lonely area layered with a calmness that had rested for centuries without activity.

A warm, dry breeze rippled across Roxy's body when she climbed out of the backseat. Kom remained silent as he leaned against the fender and lit a cigarette. His eyes followed the girlish curves of his passenger as she walked in the bright sun toward the rim of the burial pit. He knew it would be foolish to show his desires for the young American girl in the present circumstances.

Roxy scooted down the narrow path of the steep, rocky incline leading to the bottom of the shallow ravine. She had seen many shrines honoring sacred animals in Egyptian temples, but had never visited the largest of the bull sanctuaries that were before her. The hollows carved into the side of the ravine were cavernous with sturdy stone supports overhead. The mummified bulls had been stolen long ago, probably burned by the natives for fuel. There was nothing royal-looking or sacred left in the neglected area except for a few hieroglyphs barely distinguishable to an untrained eye.

While the place could excite the mind of an imaginative explorer who may be turned on by the lore of sacred animal worship, it was a site dismissed by most explorers, who craved more glamorous diggings. Roxy sensed the fascination it offered Bradford, an undertaking all his own, away from the seasoned professors who hired him as a surveyor.

The local investigators insisted the site had been searched and no suspicious clues were found. The scorching summer winds had eliminated evidence of any recent sightseers. There was no sign at all of human beings. If Kom could be believed, it was as if Bradford had been carried off by the breeze.

Roxy extended the metal pointer she carried in the pocket of her khakis, shaking the low weeds as she peered into the shadows of the caves. She had heard that small, horned serpents with poisonous bites still existed in Egypt. One might only suffer pain and sickness from the sting of a yellow scorpion, but a bite from the horned viper was usually fatal. The silence of the rocky formations was haunting and Roxy suddenly felt very alone.

The carved-out caves and the well-formed rock overhangs aroused the junior archaeologist's curiosity, but that was for another time. Her mind jerked back to the purpose at hand when she spied a small, black, plastic container lying in the scruffy weeds. Picking up the empty container, she noted its similarity to Bradford's type of film. Roxy squeezed it firmly while conjuring up visions of Brad. She combed the arid ground, but the dry, stubby weeds offered nothing more.

Even though her broad-brimmed hat shaded her, Roxy's face was flushed. Perspiration evaporated immediately in the blistering air and one could often forget the importance of water. The light-headedness that came over her alerted her to sit and open the canteen at her side. She felt giddy from early signs of dehydration as well as from a gnawing feeling that something sinister had happened to her colleague.

Roxy suddenly had the urge to leave this place of graves and get to her own safe room where she could hide in sleep, masking the dangers in this foreign land so far from home. The peril of probing in collapsing tombs was exhilarating, but the mysterious disappearance of a good friend had faded the whole summer experience for her.

Roxy's limbs felt heavy as she trudged up the craggy incline. The white heat of the sun drained the small figure as she forced herself to shuffle the two hundred yards toward the car with a dozing driver behind the wheel.

Kom squinted at the approaching girl. He was no longer in the mood to make advances toward the shapely blonde. It was lunchtime and he was ready to go home and get out of the heat. Kom stretched and turned the ignition key as Roxy sank feebly into the backseat.

"Did you find something about your friend?"

"Nothing," answered Roxy. Clearly, this was not a place to discuss her fears. "Please call me if you think of anything that might help us."

Kom opened the glove compartment and reached for a notepad, eager to take down Roxy's telephone number. Maybe the girl liked him after all and wanted to hear from him.

Roxy froze as she stared at the mechanical pencil in the glove compartment. She could not stop herself from blurting out, "That pencil, where did you get it?"

"It was in the backseat of my taxi. A passenger forgot it. Do you like it?" Kom's nerves were cool; however, he knew now that taking the pencil was a mistake.

"It's nice, like the kind we use in the tombs." Roxy's insides quivered. Brad was the only person she knew with that type of surveyor's marker; it was unique and he rarely let anyone use it. She quickly dropped the subject and took a deep breath, growing eager to distance herself from the cab driver. Kom appeared unruffled. There was no proof of anything. He often found items in his car that passengers absently left behind. The American girl was too nosey. She was a foolish foreigner playing detective in the desert. Not good to have this passenger. Kom did not want trouble.

Roxy chattered nervously about scenery and other trifling topics, hoping to appear unconcerned. She bit into the hard roll that she had stuffed in her bag. Her stomach was churning.

The ride back to town seemed endless. Roxy sighed a silent prayer when they arrived in front of the Nefertari. She handed Kom a tip with a cool goodbye as she quickly turned into the hotel. Immediately her thoughts focused on finding

Professor Semaine. She didn't go far before she spied Valerie and Surry in the drab dining area having lunch and discussing the current events.

Roxy's strained smile showed relief. "Am I ever glad to see you! That creepy cab driver has Brad's surveyor pencil. Said he found it in his backseat," she blurted. "Brad always kept that pencil safely in his buttoned shirt pocket; it wouldn't fall out by itself!"

"Settle down, Roxy, there's a lot going on here. Let's go for a walk...we can't talk here."

"And look what I found at the bull pits," gushed Roxy, pulling the plastic film container from her pocket. "Brad was there all right; it's the kind of film he uses!"

The three Americans left the stuffy hotel lobby and walked along the Nile's palm-lined pathway. They were armed for the late afternoon heat with brimmed hats and bottled water. The natives usually stayed indoors for a long nap after lunch, taking advantage of the coolness of their stone floors and thick adobe walls. From two o'clock to six the streets were generally quiet.

Shutting down during summer afternoons was a useful tradition in Mediterranean countries where the harsh heat could easily steal one's energy for the rest of the day. Tourists had to learn by experience to stay indoors until five o'clock when the natives began to stir again.

"Let's sit over there," motioned Surry. "We're lucky...at night the benches are full."

The view of the Nile was tranquil this time of the afternoon while the lethargic felucca owners napped under the sails of their anchored boats. Ferry crossings were at a minimum in the middle of the day, leaving the river gracefully smooth and almost void of traffic. Surry liked seeing the Nile calm and uncluttered, imagining how it looked in ancient times. He gazed across at the natural pyramid-shaped mountain in the distance that arose among the peaks that surrounded the distant Valley of the Kings. He felt at home in this exotic country despite the problems of the modern world.

"Roxy, I don't want you going anywhere alone from now on. It was courageous to go check on Brad today, but I would have stopped you if I knew where you were going alone. This is a friendly county, but when there's trouble the natives stick with their own people. Can't say I blame them. The Luxor police don't seem to put a high priority on Brad's disappearance. I don't see any progress at all. Human life is regarded less seriously here…a whole different philosophy. A representative from the American Embassy is coming to advise us and Brad's brother will be here soon."

Valerie stared blankly at the ground. "If Brad were sick, he would have contacted us by now. I am having grim thoughts."

"I think that grimy cab driver knows more about all this than he lets on. I don't trust him." Roxy was still shaky from the morning's ride.

"There are other concerns, Roxy. Disturbing developments about the new tomb. I get the feeling that Bassit wants to push us out of the picture and claim credit. He's dragging his feet about bringing the big boys from Cairo. Insists we stay quiet until we have a more stable entrance for the bureaucrats. Seems like lots of stalling for a discovery of this importance. Word is going to get out."

Valerie was solemn. "We've been coming to Egypt for years and I've never felt this uncomfortable about being here. The terrorist hits were worry enough and now that we've uncovered something significant, I feel even more ill at ease. Did you tell Roxy about the missing artifacts?"

"That's another puzzle. Photographs indicate that a couple of small statues have disappeared since Bassit and I documented the burial chamber. The inspector practically accused me of taking them. Unless Bassit is lying, someone else has been in there!"

Rosy took a long drink from her water bottle. "Weird,' she mused. "Do you believe in a curse about disturbing ancient tombs?"

"Not really. Do you, Roxy?" answered Surry with a faint smile.

"Guess not, but I've felt uneasy lately. I'm spooked!"

"We're all on edge about Brad. Who wouldn't be?" soothed Valerie, although she herself was not thoroughly convinced that a "tomb curse" was mere nonsense. They had been plagued by trouble recently.

"Stay cool, ladies, enough about curses. It's time to get serious about finding Brad, as well as protecting our interests in the West Valley," stated Surry tersely as he stood up with renewed energy. "I'll call The American Ambassador and get his fix on things."

The afternoon heat was stifling and the trio walked in the shade of the trees, stopping to stock up on bottled water from a young Egyptian sitting beside a battered ice chest. The dark-skinned boy with large white teeth was eager for business and was peddling his wares before the older street vendors ventured out in the heat. It was customary to haggle on the price no matter how minor the purchase.

The twirling overhead fans in the Nefertari's lobby felt good as the Americans entered. "Any messages?" asked Surry as he passed the reception desk.

"A call for you, Doctor," answered Amed. "The man would not leave his name. He will call back."

"We'll be in our room. Put the call straight through."

Surry cast a worried look toward Valerie. "I hope it's news about Bradford."

"Let me know if you hear anything." Roxy's tone was more optimistic. "I'm going for a cool shower before dinner."

"I'm fed up with delays on the announcement of the tomb, whether intentional or not." Surry said sharply. "Let's eat on the terrace tonight so we can talk without being heard."

The telephone rang as Surry turned the key in the lock. He pushed open the door and grabbed the phone. "Semaine here."

Charles Blumfield's voice was unmistakable. "It's been a while, Surry. I've been hearing lots of rumors."

"Like what, Charles?" Surry barked, skipping the formalities.

"Such as a hoard of artifacts...maybe even a royal tomb. I have friends there, you know."

"Well, yes, we've made some progress, but nothing's confirmed yet. I plan to give you a report when we verify the findings. I've been distracted by the disappearance of a close friend."

"Egypt's full of complications, Surry. Nothing new about that."

"I certainly didn't expect my surveyor to disappear! Could be foul play. The American Embassy is looking into it."

"He'll probably show up with a big adventure story for you, but what have you found so far in the West Valley? I think I have a right to be informed!" demanded Blumfield.

"The local inspector is on the site every day. He knows every step we take. Nothing's official yet, but we have come across something interesting. The Council of Antiquities is snooping around, too. They rule this place. You should know after what happened to you."

Blumfield ignored the reference to his visa fiasco. His voice escalated. "So where exactly are we now and where do I fit in? Have you forgotten who provided the map?"

Surry's jaw tightened. He had not been on the level with Blumfield, but he detested feeling guilty about the bastard. "Relax, Charles, if we keep our heads, we'll all get credit if the findings are genuine, but we've got to go along with Egyptian officials. There's no choice! I'm in contact with the American Ambassador's office about the diplomacy question. I don't want this thing to slip out of our hands any more than you do!"

"I have the feeling I'm the one slipping out of the picture, Professor. When were you going to call me? Just before the news conference?"

"This is not a time to attack each other, Charles. Let's stay cool until we confirm what's been found. You know damn well it's complicated to get things done here. If you think you can do better, come and try for yourself."

"Maybe I'll just do that! For the right price, I can get a visa. Talk to you tomorrow," he retorted, hanging up abruptly.

"Shit, all I need is Blumfield on my ass!" bellowed Surry, banging down the old-fashion black phone. "I'm about to lose it, Val. It's too much!"

Usually Surry had a deep reserve of patience, but now he was pushed to overload. With Bradford missing, a major discovery slipping away, and Charles breathing down his neck, Surry showed signs of anguish that alarmed his wife.

"Lie down, dear, I'll rub your back. We'll figure something out when you're more rested," comforted Valerie.

"Maybe if I sleep for a week it will all go away. Can't see my way through right now...the pile's too high." Surry sat listlessly on the bed, letting Valerie unbutton his shirt.

Valerie gently nudged her husband's head toward the pillow. "Try to sleep," she murmured. Within minutes, Surry was breathing deeply and was soon oblivious to the anxieties hounding him.

Disillusionment and frustration kept Valerie restless into the night. She visualized their youthful dreams fractured by the realities at hand. The whereabouts of Brad, Blumfield's nasty involvement, and the heady egos of local authorities cast cold currents on what should have been a joyous summer.

Val gave up trying to sleep and reached for her journal. Even though the cooler was blowing evenly, she felt unusually hot and the pen slipped from her clammy hand. The simple rice and cheese lunch was not settling well and her stomach churned. She glanced at Surry, hoping not to awaken him by adding to his burdens with an unwelcome illness, but with that noble thought, she bolted to the bathroom to throw up.

CHAPTER 21

Joan Kaufman was shaking with chills, fever, dysentery and dizziness within twenty-four hours after the midnight foray into the tomb with Charles. When he called to report his safe arrival in Paris, Joan's voice was weak and disoriented. Charles immediately made a call to Fatime asking him to send a doctor to check on Joan.

Dr. Abraham diagnosed flu, as food poisoning usually subsided within forty-eight hours and Joan evidently had been suffering for several days. He recommended a syrupy concoction and a diet of white rice, crackers and mint tea. Promising to return the next day, Joan was too debilitated to protest and remained in her room in a flushed stupor.

Charles called daily from his comfortable suite in Paris overlooking the majestic Place de la Concorde with the imposing Luxor Temple obelisk gleaming in the center of the city's largest square. He, too, had suffered a bout with the mysterious fever but had managed to recuperate better with the help of a confident French doctor.

After a week of foggy conversations with Charles, Joan

began to sound more coherent. "I can barely remember talking with you this past week. I'm still fragile, but my brain seems to be better. How about you?"

"Guess my siege with the tomb disease wasn't so severe, although my energy level took a hit."

"Do you think that's what this wretched bug is all about...tomb disease?"

"Tomb disease probably sounds more exotic than it really is, Joan, but there's a lot known about the effects of old bat dung and organic mold in the tombs," chuckled Charles. "When a king was buried, great amounts of food, seeds and jugs of beer were buried with him to sustain him in his underworld life. Howard Carter's entire team became seriously ill in 1922 and believed it was the Pharaoh's curse."

"Right now, I feel like I've been cursed! They'll have to pump some clean air in that cave before I set foot in it again."

"Sit tight, sweetheart. I plan to be there soon. I told Semaine to work on my visa and he knows damn well he owes me some attention. The little cheat doesn't know that I've seen his precious stash already! With the Antiquities Office acting up, he's going to need me."

"Sorry I can't give you more recent scuttlebutt, but I haven't set foot out of this hotel for days. Couldn't even talk sensibly with Fatime."

"No problem. Just get well. I'm in touch with Fatime. He said there's plenty of action in the West Valley with the team looking for the original cliff entrance. This news is about to break loose and I plan to be there when it does!"

"Hurry, I could use moral support after being a hermit lately. This is the first day I've felt strong enough to go downstairs to have dinner. Call me when you hear about your visa. Bye for now." Charles could be tender at times, mused Joan, feeling a need for affection. She rolled over and sat weakly on the side of the bed.

In a room on the floor above Joan, an alert Eric Dunn was showered, shaved and drinking coffee on his balcony as he absently eyed the Nile. It had been forty years since he vacationed in Egypt with his parents and brother, Bradford. Even before that memorable trip, Eric remembered his older brother's fascination with the golden age of Egyptian pharaohs—a curiosity that continued to amuse Brad during his lifetime. When he retired from a career as a mining surveyor, the Dunn family was happy for Bradford when he was invited to become a member of Professor Semaine's archaeological team.

Those memories were of happier times for Eric. Now the forty-six-year-old lawyer was facing more somber thoughts of his brother missing in the very desert that had given Brad great joy. Eric Dunn felt alone, tormented by dark thoughts, bewildered and out of place starring at barren hills which differed vastly from the aspen-covered Colorado Rockies that he had left behind only twenty-four hours earlier.

The past decade had not been kind to Eric. The same year that his father died, his wife was diagnosed with liver cancer. After a three-year struggle with the disease, Theresa died leaving her husband behind to raise two teenage daughters.

He was lucky to find a stouthearted, loving housekeeper who the girls respected while Eric slowly began to rebuild his life. Even though he buried himself in loads of mining cases, he often found time for weekends at the cabin in Manitou Springs to fish and hike with his daughters. Grandmother Dunn lived with the family which included the household's two golden retrievers rounding out the formula that sustained the courageous clan.

When Eric received the alarming report about Bradford he did not share his fears with the rest of the family, merely saying that he was invited to visit Uncle Brad in Egypt. His aging mother did not detect the urgency of Eric's departure. Egypt's Foreign Office had not yet issued a missing person report and there was no mention in newspapers.

After the seven-thousand-mile flight from Colorado, Eric's stomach growled in discomfort when the thick Turkish coffee finally hit. Thoughts of a decent meal and the meeting with Professor Semaine lured him off of the warm balcony to the chore of getting dressed.

Wrinkles in the gray cotton jacket went unnoticed as he slipped it over a black t-shirt. He hurriedly smoothed his dark hair with a swift hand movement, picked up keys and a wallet, and left the disheveled room, with the small suitcase on the floor only half unpacked.

His mind was fixed on the list of things to do before meeting Semaine at four o'clock. He emailed the family, carefully stating it was early morning and that he had seen no one yet and that he would send news of Brad soon. Satisfying his unsteady stomach was a priority, leaving the call to his office for later. He wondered what the Egyptian Hotel might offer for comfort food.

The maître'd in the hotel's spacious Belle Époque Restaurant led Eric to a table next to a tall window overlooking the river. It was barely noon and he was the sole diner in the room. The few tourists who braved the hot summer season had not returned from the morning bus tours and local inhabitants rarely ate in the expensive dining room.

After deciding that the raviolis would be the most settling fare for his unsteady stomach, Eric looked up from the menu, noting an attractive woman seated two tables away. Although the lady wore a flowing *jelabiya*, jade beads and silk shoes, her pale skin and fair hair signaled a foreigner. Hearing her conversation with the waiter, Eric noted a familiar American accent.

Ordinarily Joan would have noticed the nice-looking man eating alone in the huge room but her level of alertness was lagging after several days of wobbly nausea and fever. She glanced absently out the window at the *feluccas* drifting down the river.

After lunch with wine, Eric's mood lightened. He felt like talking and surprised himself by boldly approaching Joan's table. "Hello, I'm Eric Dunn from Colorado and I think we Americans should befriend each other in this far-off land. May I join you for coffee?"

Joan Kauffman was shaken from her reverie, looking startled to see a stranger smiling down at her. He was appealing enough, especially after her siege of solitude. "Well, yes, it does seem as if we're the only Americans here this afternoon. Please sit down."

The new acquaintances finished a carafe of wine before the strawberry crepes arrived. More personal information poured out than was the usual habit of either. It was clear that both travelers were in need of a friend.

Joan had heard rumors about the missing surveyor. She listened thoughtfully as Eric revealed his anxiety concerning his brother's disappearance. Neither Joan nor Eric perceived the sinister link of their chance encounter.

A certain spark entered Joan's conversation. It had been ages since she felt attracted to a complete stranger. Eric Dunn emitted a frontier ruggedness that was softened by his openness and sincere manner which Joan found particularly appealing after being with a scheming man like Charles

Blumfield.

"You've made my welcome in Egypt very pleasant, Miss Kaufman. I'm meeting Dr. Semaine at four, but I hope we can do this again while you're here."

"I would like that. I'll be staying at the hotel for a while longer. I've met Doctor Semaine, he's a brilliant man." Noting that the person she just met had gathered up her check with his own, she smiled. "Thank you, Eric, very nice of you."

Eric merely smiled, guiding her out of the deserted dining room into the thick-carpeted hallway leading to the lobby. "After I hear Semaine's ideas concerning my brother I'll call you." He looked into her eyes for what seemed like an unusually long moment and then turned and strolled out of the hotel.

Joan walked briskly up the stairs to her room. Was it the hearty lunch or was it meeting Eric Dunn that added liveliness to her step?

The last occasion that had brought the Semaines and Dunns together was a happier one years prior when Surry was guest speaker at The University of Denver. Bradford had flown in for the lecture, taking the opportunity to visit his mom and brother while proudly introducing Doctor Semaine to his family. It had been an event filled with high spirits, but now the mood between Eric Dunn and Surry Semaine was entirely different.

"Unfortunately, Eric, that's about all we know about Brad since we last saw him," stated Surry. "I wanted to fill you in before we meet with the American Attaché at dinner tonight. We hope he'll use pressure for a more intense search...right now we're at a standstill. All we have is an empty film container and a statement from Brad's cab driver."

"That guy gave me the creeps!" injected Roxy. "He had Brad's surveyor pencil that he found in the back seat of his cab...yeah, sure! The police questioned him several times but there's no proof that actually incriminates him."

Eric listened intently. "It seems strange that nothing substantial has surfaced after this long. Do you think the search at the site was thorough enough?"

"It gets touchy to question their professionalism, but they tell us they're still working on the case. Roxy and I have both looked around the abandoned bull pits and nothing except a film container was found."

"There's nothing stopping him when he wants to go on a photo shoot, but he usually plays it safe. For my own peace of mind, I've got to go to that place where he was last seen alive."

"Maybe Roxy can go with you...with a different driver, of course. I'd go too, but there's a diplomatic problem I have to clear up tomorrow. Seems like this project has been jinxed from the start."

Surry put his arm around Eric's shoulder as they walked from the terrace of the lush gardens surrounding the Winter Palace Hotel. "I know it's difficult for you Eric, but I'm relieved you're here. Plan to meet the Attaché at dinner in the Mercure Hotel at seven-thirty. My wife won't be with us; she's fighting a fever."

It was the second mention of a fever Eric had heard about that day. He had neglected to mention meeting Joan Kaufman at lunch earlier that day. Eric needed a nap. His feet felt heavy as he climbed the stairs to the second floor.

CHAPTER 22

Inspector Bassit was seething. He found it difficult to ignore Professor Semaine no matter how much he wanted the American archaeologists out of the picture. On his desk was a letter from the Ambassador of the United States specifically congratulating him and his compatriots concerning Semaine's partnership in the West Valley discovery. The letter also requested a visa for one Charles Blumfield, a philanthropist, who was willing to donate major funding for the project. Costs for restoring an ancient tomb were especially welcome during the current cut-back in Egypt's cultural funds.

A member of Cairo's Council of Antiquities met in Bassit's office to discuss the authenticity of the new discovery and the far-reaching effects if the funerary goods proved to be those of the great Herihor. There could be no question that the initial announcement of the discovery would be made by the Egyptian government; however, the need for continued financial support from the United States made it necessary to recognize the American archaeologists as well.

Blumfield's conditional visa was issued after his $250,000 donation was received by cashier's check along with the written promise of further contributions. Arabs rarely forget an insult and while it was doubtful that they would forget Blumfield's obnoxious actions in the Cairo Museum, he could be tolerated if his commitment of monetary donations proved to be genuine. Chief Bassit detested the necessity of sharing Egypt's international glory with foreigners, but their money for research was essential.

The inspector was not at all sorry that Semaine's surveyor from Colorado had disappeared; he was one less outsider to cope with. In fact, Bassit wished the Professor and his wife would conveniently disappear as well and he was fully capable of considering such ideas with seriousness.

While documenting the newly found burial goods, the American and Egyptian archaeologists continued to work side-by-side with cool courtesy. It became evident that the inventory in the burial chamber was that of the mighty Herihor. The verification accelerated the fervor of all those fortunate enough to be involved.

Surry and Bassit supervised the inventory of the burial goods while experts from Cairo explored the pits and traps of the spider-like corridors to determine the original tomb entrance. Sonar equipment was used on the outside cliffs in search of the primary entry used by Herihor's funeral cortege.

Only the smaller artifacts could be taken out through the primitive tunnel originating from the Amenhotep tomb. A public announcement had to wait until the tomb's major entryway was found, enabling safe passage to the Cairo Museum laboratory for many of the most delicate treasures. Only then could Herihor's tomb be prepared for the deluge of eager officials and media reporters chosen to view the sensational discovery.

At five-thirty in the morning, Roxy Morgan accompanied Surry to the ferry landing lined with merchants and workers heading for duties on the West Bank.

"Thanks for letting me go along today. I need to get back to work to shake off my funk about Brad," mumbled Roxy. "His brother and the Attaché are on the case now and there's little more for us to do until we hear if they find anything."

"We're both cleared to go in early today with Bassit," Surry whispered as they climbed the rickety gangplank of the old ferry. "He's become unfriendly since the project took on international important. I think he'd like us out of Luxor altogether. The only reason we're still around are the American dollars."

Surry frowned into the morning sun. "It's been tough on all of us to lose Brad just when we thought we had this big find within our grasp. If Val's health isn't better soon, I may start believing in the tomb curse myself!"

Eager to lighten the subject, Roxy's tone became impish. "Can you believe that Eric Dunn has been cozy with Joan Kaufman? I guess it's been a depressing trip for him and he welcomes someone to have dinner with…maybe breakfast, too."

"He seems like a savvy fellow. I'm sure he can take care of himself." Surry looked amused. "It's ironic that he found Kaufman of all people. I figured her for Blumfield's girl. We'll see what happens when that arrogant jerk hits town."

Bassit's assistant greeted them as they descended on the west side of the Nile. The government Jeep easily passed through checkpoints on the route to the West Valley. The monumental cliffs of the deserted canyon never failed to offer an eerie welcome no matter how many times one entered the lonely gorge. Knowing that the same winding trail had been traveled by royal burial processions three thousand years before never failed to mesmerize Surry. He was in his place. The steep walls of the canyon were filled with coves and hidden corners which might hold still more unknown treasures. Imagining how much more was hidden in those cliffs stirred Surry's blood!

The Jeep came to a dusty halt. Four trusted workers were seated crossed-legged near the entrance of Amenhotep's tomb. They had been kept for menial chores, but were no longer allowed inside the tomb. The turbaned men stood up from their huddle, welcoming the Professor with extending hands and toothy smiles. They made no effort to acknowledge Roxy.

It was no secret among the small crew that there was mysterious activity in the tunnel that angled from the main tomb, but they knew better than to allow curiosity to jeopardize the weekly pay envelope as they went about keeping the outside area orderly. Surry routinely scanned the premises before heading for the chamber that consumed his thoughts.

Surry and Roxy followed Rachid inside the cool cavern. "Chief Bassit will come soon and we may know today if the surveyors are right about locating Herihor's main entrance," remarked the inspector. "I will go first to make certain the generator and lights function. I will send the 'all clear' signal."

"Let me go in next," pleaded the impatient girl. "I've been left out of all this intrigue for too long!" It was a disastrous request to go in next and it would prove to be her last. From inside the dark hole, Surry and Roxy heard the generator cough into life.

Inside the tunnel Rachid switched on the string of tiny

lights that lined the corridor. He then carried out Bassit's
heinous instructions by placing a small burlap sack midway
in the dim passageway, cautiously emptying the bag and
hastily darting toward the new burial chamber with the
empty sack in his pocket.

Roxy's flashlight bounced along the shadows of the
jagged walls as she awkwardly crawled along the passage.
She was exhilarated to be back at work. She could make out
the faint glow from the chamber ahead which enlivened her
progress. She did not notice the rapid movement of the
small horned serpent as it slid onto her boot, clamping its
tiny mouth onto her leg. Roxy's scream echoed throughout
the tunnel as she felt the sharp stinging puncture.

"What happened? I'm coming!" Surry called anxiously
from a short distance behind Roxy. His lantern caught the
girl's silhouette leaning weakly against the wall.

"Snake bite...over there," she murmured, pointing
limply to the remains of the venomous creature that she had
pounded off with her flashlight. Partially crushed, it had
done its damage. The terrified girl's rush of adrenalin
hurried the noxious venom though her veins.

The *cerastes cornutus*, commonly known as the horned
viper, has existed in the Middle East for thousands of years.
The little creature is usually less than twelve inches long and
has the distinguishing feature of a tiny reptilian horn above
each eye. In Pharaonic times the slippery little beasts were
revered along with cobra as guardians of the underworld.
Replicas of both species often show up in early tomb wall
drawings. Legend has it that Cleopatra VII enlisted the
poisonous viper to bring about her infamous suicide in 30
B.C.

Although the deadly serpent prefers marshy terrains near
rivers and canals, occasionally they can be found in nearby

caves and tombs. It is not known to be aggressive but when agitated or attacked the viper's venom is lethal.

"I'm scared," the young woman gasped, her dry lips barely moving.

"Don't talk, Roxy. I'll get you out of here fast. We'll get anti-venom serum!" Surry strained to keep his voice calm as he carefully maneuvered Roxy from the tunnel. His heart palpitated as he remembered the anti-venom kit in Valerie's backpack which was at the hotel. Surry knew enough not to apply a tourniquet or make an incision. He could only try to reassure his wounded friend.

Rachid followed the frantic pair out of the tomb, running ahead to start the Jeep. "There's a clinic in the West Village," he said nervously, watching Surry place Roxy's head on his lap in the backseat. "They know about snake bites. I picked up the dead snake for identification." Roxy's fateful attacker lay lifeless in a cloth bag on the floor of the speeding vehicle. The Arab's face was stoic, concealing his fury that the wrong victim had been stricken. His orders had been to rid the world of the American professor, not the insignificant female student.

Roxy was silent, her eyes glazed. Her fingers shook slightly, but she no longer spoke. Surry found himself murmuring prayers for the first time in years while he gently stroked Roxy's clammy forehead. "Pray that this clinic has the right serum, Rachid. There's no time to cross the river!"

Rachid stopped the Jeep with a jerk and Surry carried Roxy through the stark white waiting room crammed with veiled women, whimpering babies, and ailing children. Men needing care waited outside of the mud-brick structure.

Surry tenderly laid the girl on a simple wooden cot covering her flushed body with a thin blanket. In a trance he leaned against the wall while the doctor jabbed a syringe into the arm of the motionless form.

Doctor Fara was the only certified doctor in his native village. He had been a gifted student, winning a scholarship to London University where he succeeded in becoming the first in his family to graduate from medical school. With determination and purpose he returned to the village of his ancestors armed with a grant to establish a valid medical facility in the small community. Fara was adequately knowledgeable about current medicines and cures but was continually frustrated by lack of funds, inadequate supplies and too many patients. The overcrowded clinic depended upon small amounts of aid from the government and income from the few paying tourists who showed up for emergency treatment.

"I must tell you, sir, I have seen only one man survive a horned viper attack, and he was a large native with weathered skin," announced the dignified doctor with a British accent.

Doctor Fara injected a second dose of serum into Roxy's limp arm. "The deadly venom spreads quickly. May God be with her," he added solemnly.

Surry crouched beside the cot, lowering his head in his hands. A heavy darkness faded the world around him. He felt sick to his stomach. Short, uneven breaths came from the helpless woman whose color had paled.

Reaching for her hand, Surry remained by her side with his eyes closed, wishing somehow he could relay his strength for her fight to survive. He looked up at the Doctor. "Please call Luxor to see if they have other antidotes. I must get her across the river."

"Yes, we must try everything. I will tell them you are coming," responded Fara in an even tone.

Wrapped in a thin coverlet, Roxy was carried to the

Jeep's backseat. Surry held her on his lap. "Take the bridge; we can't wait for a ferry. Floor this thing!"

The car sped along the smooth new asphalt toward the high-tech bridge. Rachid's official vehicle was recognized and was waived through the checkpoints. Surry fought to quell his panic as he listened to the frail figure's weak spurts of breath that were slowly becoming less audible.

CHAPTER 23

When the Jeep carrying Roxy raced past the Winter Place Hotel toward the Luxor Hospital that morning, the shutters of Joan Kaufman's river view suite had not yet been opened. Inside she and Eric Dunn were oblivious to noise from the street or to anything else beyond their own pleasures.

Joan smiled as Eric approached the bed carrying a cup of coffee from the mirrored mini-bar. She had a lot to smile about. Their friendly dinners in the hotel's restaurant had become a regular occurrence, easing the lonely boredom of the sparsely filled hotel. Time zones and emotions can become surreal among fellow countrymen who are displaced on foreign soil, allowing intimacy and trust to develop at accelerated speeds.

Eric found himself discussing Theresa's death with Joan, a topic he rarely shared with others. While describing his teen-age daughters, he admitted his insecurities as a single father—feelings he had stubbornly hidden, even from himself. Eric's mask of forced optimism fell away while Joan listened attentively to his worst fears about his missing brother.

The bottles of French wine uncorked during their dinners produced confessions that had fermented for years. Joan's guard melted away as she sheepishly revealed her long entanglement with a married man, even admitting her clandestine scouting duties concerning Professor's Semaine's project.

Eric was not particularly disturbed by his dinner partner's sleuthing activities. In his world of legal mischief, snooping tactics were commonplace. Discussing the bizarre proceedings surrounding the American project was of more interest to Eric. Until recently he looked upon archaeology as a fascinating hobby. He was beginning to realize how pitifully naïve he had been about the economics of tourism and the world market for ancient artifacts. Much of Egypt's economy depended upon the parade of tourists flocking to see the historical sites, while the livelihood of thousands of other citizens revolved around the trade in antiquities, whether real or fake.

Floundering in a strange country fuels the need for sympathetic companionship and the posh hotel's Royal Bar was an ideal haven for Eric and Joan to share their worries over brandy. The bond was sealed late one night when the two hungry souls progressed upstairs, devouring each other after the door closed and Joan's caftan slipped to the floor. By morning their burdens seemed easier to bear.

"I would say we make a good pair. What do you think, Miss Joan?"

Joan's eyes softened as she reached for the coffee cup in Eric's hand. "All I can think about at the moment is that I'm very happy to be here with you," she said in a soft tone which was without the sharp edge of ambition usually noticeable in her voice.

Eric stretched out on the bed beside her. "I would have

been a pitiful man in Egypt without you, Joan. Having you here has meant a lot to me." Joan reached over and pulled Eric closer. "It all seems unreal, doesn't it?" They lay entwined in each other's arms and drifted into the safety of sleep.

A jolting ring interrupted their drowsy contentment. The loud, confident voice of Charles Blumfield was unmistakable. "Well, Joanie, it won't be long before I'm in Luxor legally. My visa has cleared. I told you I could swing it!"

"Oh, sorry, Charles…guess I fell asleep after breakfast. You'll be here…when?"

"Wake up, Joan. Time to make plans. I'll be there in three days. Have you missed me?"

"Sure…sure, Charles. We'll talk when you get here. Call when you land in Cairo."

"You okay? Over your fever? You sound foggy. Better get some rest before I get there. This Herihor thing is about to explode! We'll have some celebrating to do. Must go, babe, lots to do."

Joan slowly hung up the phone. A helpless glaze overshadowed the sparkle that had been in her eyes earlier. She reached over without a word and squeezed Eric's hand.

"Sounds like troubles," Eric said gently.

Her head sunk into the pillow, her eyes fixed on the ceiling. "Yes, difficulties of my own making. Terrible time for Charles to arrive! Last night scrambled my emotions."

"Well, my mind's clear on the matter. I don't like the guy already and I hope he's not planning to move in with you," barked Eric uncharacteristically. An awkward silence surrounded the couple lying in a bed still warm with memories.

The sudden coldness Joan felt toward Charles was

frightening. Eric Dunn had managed to thoroughly distort feelings she had lived with for years. Her head felt heavy and, closing her eyes, she searched the darkness for clarity.

"You evidently have some thinking to do, my dear." Eric's voice was curt. "I'm going to my room to shower and shave before my lunch with the American Attaché. We'll talk at dinner."

"This has been so fast, Eric. Suddenly I want Charles out of my life." She watched Eric pull off the towel as he took brisk steps across the room. The memory of her hands on that firm, bare derrière stirred her. With this man she experienced a girlish glee that had become dormant in recent years. Knowing Eric had illuminated a fresh future for Joan.

CHAPTER 24

It was unusual for Surry Semaine to shed tears. He was not a sullen man even though his nature often appeared to be on the serious side. Roxy's death shattered him. His nerves, already taut from Bradford's disappearance, Valerie's illness and tomb troubles, finally gave way in the waiting room of Luxor's modest hospital. With his head in his hands, he sobbed like a lost child.

A sickening jumble of breakfast swirled inside his stomach. Even his thinking was muddled. Perhaps the tomb carried a curse after all. Perhaps the dead do not want to be disturbed by the living? Surry lowered his head to his knees. He breathed deeply, steadying the wooziness that churned within. "Breathe, Surry...breathe in courage," he told himself. He had responsibilities. Roxy's parents must be notified, Valerie had to be told and his crumbling career needed attention.

With resolve Surry raised himself from the wooden bench in the bleak corridor and entered the cubicle where Roxy's lifeless body lay. Surry glared unblinkingly at the pasty white body of his young assistant, now totally void of the cheerful vitality that had filled it only hours before.

Surry remembered guiding Roxy toward her career in archaeology and taking pride in her successes, and now…this promising life had been snuffed out. Maybe if he had entered the tunnel first he would have seen the snake? Perhaps his larger frame could have survived the poison? Clouds of guilt rolled over him. He had been careless about bringing the venom kit, even though the medics said it would have done little good for a bite by a horned viper. Again he felt lightheaded. Leaning against the wall next to Roxy's cot, he reached over and smoothed her limp blonde hair. The coolness of her face startled him. He knew Roxy was no longer there.

The doctor stood at the doorway of the gloomy room. "I'm sorry, Monsieur Semaine, we could do nothing more for your friend. This viper brings death quickly. How shall we prepare the body? Will it be shipped to America?"

Surry winced. Shipped? Like merchandise to be laid in the hands of her parents? He stiffened. "I'll call her home today for instructions. Miss Morgan will be accompanied to the United States." He realized it was his own distant voice that spoke the words. Walking numbly into the dusty street, he continued on foot to the Nefertari Hotel. He needed to be with Valerie.

Valerie's cold chills had subsided but the irritating rash was still a bother. For the first time in several days she got out of bed contemplating a cool shower. She was startled to see Surry enter the room, sullen and pale.

His somberness alarmed her. "My fever's gone, dear, I'm feeling better…are you sick now? What's wrong?" She watched her husband mechanically tug at his boot.

He stretched out on the bed with his eyes closed. "I've got to lie down."

"If it's bad news from home, tell me!" Valerie demanded fearfully.

Rolling over on his side, he stared at his wife. "It's not about the kids. It's here."

Valerie's body relaxed. She could cope with a career crisis easier than a family calamity. Wrapping her arms around her distraught mate, she watched his eyes glisten with tears.

"Roxy was bitten by a viper. We couldn't save her. She died an hour ago."

"Oh my God," gasped Val, rolling flat on her back, her eyes closed tightly.

CHAPTER 25

A flurry of communications flowed between the U.S. Embassy in Cairo and Cairo's Office of Foreign Affairs. Tragic mishaps involving two American archaeologists in such a short period of time signaled alarm. Now Professor Semaine's personal safety was in question and any further accidents could prove problematic for diplomatic relations. Two Marine sergeants from the United States Embassy Security Division were dispatched to accompany the Semaines during the remainder of their stay in Egypt.

Grudgingly, Chief Inspector Bassit continued to include the American professor in the Herihor Tomb exploration events. He arrogantly informed Surry that a possible entrance to the great Pharaoh's tomb had been located in a hillside above the tomb of Amenhotep and invited him to join officials on the following morning for an inspection of the corridor leading from Herihor's burial chamber through a passage leading to a possible main entrance.

It was welcome news. The thought of being in the presence of the king's treasures again lightened Surry's dark mood. He had been in low spirits since Valerie left for Ohio to accompany Roxy Morgan's coffin. Surry suffered from an unshakable fatigue that had kept him languishing in gloom for days.

Before dawn, Surry dutifully dressed and joined Bassit's team in the West Valley tomb. The crew of experts had high hopes for verification of the original entry used by Herihor's funeral cortege. Lacking his usual strength, Surry mechanically followed the group through the decorated corridor leading away from Heritor's sarcophagus. The newly located passageway extending from the room where the huge coffin lay was nearly ten feet wide in a straight alignment typical of twentieth-dynasty royal tombs. A stale mineral smell filled Surry's nostrils, an intoxicating odor of the mysterious underworld that was known to have the ability to mesmerize intruders.

Surry willingly surrendered his imagination to the lure of imposing gods and goddesses who were pictured marching along the ancient stone walls. These same painted figures had welcomed the Pharaoh's immense granite sarcophagus during the pageantry of the royal funeral procession thirty centuries ago.

Renewed energy surged within Surry as his addiction to pharaonic legend took over his senses. Drifting from the troubled world of the twenty-first century, Surry rode on his dreams to Egypt's golden era with visions of the magnificent parade of priests transporting the mummified king to a final underworld home.

Scholars have found numerous references in tombs and temple hieroglyphs describing the public highlights of royal burials suggesting that the high priests verbally passed on the secret burial rituals to only a few privileged clerics. Papyrus scrolls pertaining to other ancient religious interment ceremonies have been found, but only a few pictorial images in obscure holy places give insight into the precise final events of a pharaoh's interment.

In early times the news of a pharaoh's death traveled rapidly by word-of-mouth, plunging the entire Egyptian population into mourning. Because the almighty ruler was considered the direct link between the gods and the people, the connection was dangerously disrupted when the king died. If the proper prayers and offerings were not made, disorder in heaven could cause havoc on earth.

Preparation for the pharaoh's journey to join other heavenly gods was a serious and strict tradition of procedures. Every burial detail had to be performed meticulously so the gods could continue to be involved in order to prevent the world from being thrown off balance. Fastidious care of the king's body during the mummification process lasted exactly seventy days before priests could transfer the purified mummy into the prepared tomb where the deceased king would begin his life of eternity in the underworld.

If a pharaoh died unexpectedly after a short reign, tomb workers had only a seventy-day period to prepare his tomb before the mummy arrived. Several royal tombs in the Valley of the King, such as the tomb of the young Tutankhamen, were left in a modified or unfinished status when workers had to be dismissed after the official mourning period and the king's body was ready to be laid to rest. Only high priests, family members and a few trusted nobles were allowed to accompany the mummy into the tomb for final prayers and the sealing ceremony.

King Tutankhamen died prematurely—some historians speculate that he was murdered—at age nineteen when the work on his tomb was in the preliminary stage. A hasty substitute was quickly prepared for the burial of the young ruler's mummy. Although Tutankhamen's tomb is currently one of the most famous, it is actually the smallest enclosure of all the known kings in the royal acropolis. There is a common belief among scholars that Tut's magnificent burial treasury is insignificant compared to hieroglyphic descriptions of more important pharaohs. The impressive golden artifacts of a minor king like Tut allow experts to calculate the fantastic wealth that must have existed in the tombs of powerful kings such as Ramses II and Amenhotep III before looting took place.

A king's embalming ritual consisted of extravagant and precise ceremonies scheduled every day during the seventy days of official mourning. Special prayers, strict diets, symbolic apparel and daily temple rites were rigorously imposed on the royal family and priests. While the king's body was being drained of fluids on a slanted marble altar, his liver, lungs, stomach and intestines were removed and placed in aromatic spices to dry. When completely dehydrated, the organs were individually wrapped in fine linen and placed in four separate alabaster canopic jars.

The parched king's cadaver was symbolically cleansed numerous times and anointed with sacred oils and herbs. Small linen bags filled with the salt-like powder called natron and were then inserted into the body to further the drying process. The outer skin of the king was puffed up with resin-soaked linens for a more lifelike appearance. Painted ivory or colored glass eyes were inserted into the eye sockets before the embalmed cadaver was placed on the marble slab to continue drying for another thirty days.

The strict steps of the body's purification were carried out in the holiest of temples with only an elite core of holy men and family allowed to observe. Recitations, spells, offerings and reverent chants continued in every other sacred shrine in Egypt to honor the deceased ruler during the seventy-day period.

To begin its journey to the final resting place, the monarch's encased mummy was loaded onto a gilded sledge at the sanctified temple where the purification ritual had taken place. The newly designated king led the parade of costumed priests, followed by the royal wooden sledge carrying the inner coffin. Directly behind the casket other priests carried an elaborate chest containing the four sealed canopic jars containing the deceased pharaoh's mummified entrails. Each jar was topped with a sculpted lid—three in the shape of animal heads and one in the shaped of a human head.

Masked ministers, influential priests, distinguished viziers and family members were all transported across the Nile in spectacular royal barges which followed the high priest in the leading royal vessel carrying the dead pharaoh. The riverbanks swarmed with grieving Egyptians who gathered from miles around to pay homage as the funeral flotilla glistened in the rays of the setting sun as it floated toward the imperial necropolis.

More nobles with champion oxen were waiting on the West Bank ready to pull the sledges with the mummified king and other underworld necessities up the winding route to the sacred city of the dead where the prepared tomb awaited the imperial entourage.

Visions of Herihor's lavish funeral procession marched through Surry's head as the beam of his light flickered along the adorned figures chiseled on the walls of the passage. He was oblivious to the others in Bassit's group who trudged in front of him while his thoughts fused with the musty smells luring him into a dreamlike spell from Egypt's glorious past. Surry's own sorrows were conveyed within him as he magically merged with the grieving line of mourners following the king's coffin traveling toward the world of the dead. The cheerless crowd led by ancient priests was followed by an entranced Surry Semaine.

It was in the sanctified vault where the closing stages of the entombment took place including a grand funerary feast for privileged mourners in the adjacent pillared chamber. Leftovers from the banquet plus containers of preserved food, wine and beer were blessed and deposited in the side storage rooms for the dead king's afterlife requirements. Exquisitely-tailored clothing, jewelry, perfumes, weapons, games, musical instruments, bed linens, tableware, chests, chairs, beds and sentimental mementoes were also placed in storage for use in the king's next life. Religious icons and statues of animal gods were strategically put in niches for assurance that the ruler's mummy would be taken care of in its new world of rebirth.

Hundreds of small stone or wooden *shabti* figures were positioned near the coffin, representing magical workers to assist the pharaoh in the underworld kingdom. Miniature tools, trays of planted seeds, a full size chariot, plows and grinding stones, were also supplied for the afterlife entourage.

When the mourners' feast ended and the funeral goods were properly placed in their designated places, only then was the most momentous of the major rites ready to take place. The most holy function was performed by the new pharaoh as the final act before the mummy was officially sealed in the granite sarcophagus. A bronze prod was inserted through the linen bandages into the mummy's mouth depositing a magic mixture of herbs for the purpose of reawakening the physical senses of the body and restoring animation to the lifeless cadaver.

The wrapped sovereign's mummified body was again anointed with incense and spices while nestled in its golden anthropoid casket before being placed in a second larger wooden coffin and then in an alabaster case which was then lowered, with the help of ropes and pulleys, into the giant sarcophagus. The chief priest ordered the heavy granite lid to be placed on top and proceeded to ceremoniously apply the regal cartouches.

Prayers and offerings continued while the funeral party backed out of the long dark passageway, terminating the lengthy event with the application of the imperial clay seals on the thick wooden block at the outside entrance. Heavy mounds of debris and boulders were put in place to disguise the location of the tomb. When sufficiently hidden, an elite sentry squadron was posted on the cliffs to guard the general vicinity day and night.

Normally a pharaoh's tomb could not be unsealed except to receive the mummy of an important royal family member, such as a favorite wife or son, but only if the king had specifically requested such an occurrence in his last testament.

Early court scrolls document reports concerning the pillaging of treasure-filled tombs shortly after interment of the king by disloyal construction workers or guards. If robbers were caught in this sacrilegious act, they were put to death after a speedy trial. Centuries later during the Greek and Roman occupation, when the capital of Egypt was moved from Thebes, later known as Luxor, to Alexandria, the tombs in the Valley of the Kings were poorly guarded and soon became a hunting ground for professional looters. To this day it is believed by historians that not all of the regal tombs have been found.

In the second century A.D., when Christianity began to

spread into Egypt, the pharaonic temples and tombs were seen as disrespectful pagan symbols. Christians were encouraged to destroy or deface the temples and palaces of pharaohs and use what remained of the magnificent structures as holy chapels or churches.

Appreciation for the sophisticated culture of Egypt's dynastic era did not have a firm revival until Napoleon Bonaparte invaded the region with his French army and intellectual *savants* in 1798. Napoleon's team of scholars returned to France loaded with artifacts, sketches and enthusiastic tales of miraculous sights, which generated great interest throughout Europe. From then on the wonders of Ancient Egypt influenced European furniture makers, fashion designers, artists, fabric mills and rug manufacturing in the nineteenth century, a fascination which developed into a world-wide frenzy after Howard Carter discovered Tutankhamen's tomb in 1922.

In a trance, Surry Semaine envisioned himself in the somber funeral parade of Herihor's mourners. The figures of gods of the underworld carved on the walls of the tomb's main passageway did not appear ominous to him as he mechanically trudged along in a dreamy euphoria. In fact, Surry was untroubled by the idea of following the pharaoh's mummy into the afterlife, where he might once again be with Roxy and Bradford Dunn.

A sense of vast timelessness enveloped Surry, diluting his worries of the present day. Hovering in the illusionary spell, nothing seemed to matter except the shadowy sensation of fantasy that surrounded him. He longed to remain in the painless delirium forever, to lose himself in this vague world of lost civilization.

Bassit's austere voice shattered his reverie, jolting Surry back to reality in the musty corridor. It was so brief, that vivid journey into past centuries. *Like the brevity of life itself*, thought the dazed Professor.

Bassit's team halted before the outline of a massive wooden barricade. A wave of excitement rippled through the small contingent of authorities standing silently in the poorly-lit cave. "This partition faces east. If we are correct in our calculations, this will be the main entrance," announced the Inspector.

The group stood spellbound as Bassit's light shone on the impressive figures kneeling devoutly on either side of the huge hinged barrier. The life-size identical sculptures were carved in stone relief bending in homage to Re, the all-important Sun God, represented by a gold gilt solar disc. High priests considered it imperative that a dead king pay tribute to the Sun God immediately upon entering his newly prepared afterlife dwelling to assure that the mummy's soul would be awakened each morning at sunrise to rule with the other gods over heaven and earth.

Ceilings of the twenty-first-dynasty tombs typically painted a pharaoh's name and likeness in unison with the Solar God's heavenly journey across the sky as ruler of the universe. The symbol of the Sun God, customarily shining with thick gold leaf, was prominently displayed in the entrances of Royal New Kingdom tombs, which always faced the rising sun. Osiris, the ruling God of the Underworld, was depicted deeper in the tomb as one proceeded west toward the setting sun.

Imposing wall reliefs of gods, royal figures and magical animals lined the route that the majestic coffin had passed on its journey to the burial chamber. Skillfully-chiseled instructions and test questions were present at each gate along the downward path in order to enlighten the dead king about the guidelines of a successful afterlife. A flamboyantly-decorated procession covered the stone walls on the way to the king's resting place. Images included an abundance of ornate depictions of the deceased pharaoh paying homage to the gods and offering appropriate gifts to numerous underworld deities.

The group that accompanied Bassit stood transfixed as they came face-to-face with the artistry of an ancient society which hinted of a higher level of sophistication than their own current lifestyle. For a moment the petty jealousies between the experts seemed diminished in the mesmerizing atmosphere of past genius.

"Soon we shall share this splendid discovery of Egypt's heritage with the world," whispered Bassit, his eyes awestruck by the brilliant art on the walls before him. When he focused on the American professor, a look of distain crossed his features, as if the momentous occasion was marred by the presence of the foreigner. "We cannot allow news of this to be known until the authorities from Cairo have observed this."

The fading hope that the American team would be honored in the discovery was growing dim in Surry's mind. His lifelong dream began to wane in a wave of nauseating disappointment.

CHAPTER 26

Blumfield's reappearance in Luxor was awkward for all the people he knew except for his driver Fatime. Assignments from Charles were a boost to Fatime's livelihood and, even though they appeared to be a questionable team, the association worked well for both parties. Fatime had resources that could deliver almost any request without the bothersome discussion of morals or consequences. Charles and his lackey understood each other. The loyalty of Blumfield's female ally in Luxor had faded. Joan Kaufman's romance with Eric Dunn muddled her previous romantic feelings, leaving her mind in a jumble of confusion.

"You should level with the guy, Joan," Eric said gently at dinner that evening. "What we have together is more than a summer fling…at least for me it is."

"Stop it, Eric. lease know you are very important to me. It's just that Charles has been in my life for many years and he won't be graceful about being asked to disappear."

"Remember he's a married man, my dear. I think it's

about time you stop being a spy for him, as well as an accomplice in his other unsavory ideas."

Eric's openness appealed to Joan; nevertheless, his words stung. "Try not to be angry with me. All this has happened fast and it's an awkward mess."

"Well, one thing's for certain, he's arriving tomorrow and if he moves in with you, I'll be understandably disgusted." Eric reached for the wine, straining to control his agitation.

"Ridiculous! Charles won't be moving in with me. At least I owe him the courtesy of explaining the current situation. Be patient, Eric, I'll work it out, I promise." Her eyes misted with frustration.

Eric took a deep breath and leaned back in the chair. "Sorry, but if there's a future for us, it cannot include Blumfield. I'm not up to dealing with a love triangle."

"Don't get mean, Eric. There's no love triangle and I would like to think you and I have a future together."

"Perhaps I am being harsh in my frankness. Guess my emotions have been jerked around too much lately."

Joan nervously pushed the pasta around on her plate as she looked across at Eric's boyish face. "It's a distasteful problem, I know, but I'll do whatever it takes to get us through this." Her feelings were in the open now and Eric's naturalness made Joan more aware than ever how much she liked this man. Dealing with the darkness surrounding Charles was a duty she dreaded.

Eric's hand reached over covering hers. "I'll try to be patient, but after we solve things here, let's go back to the States together. What do you think?"

Lightness washed over Joan, wringing out a grin. "I'd like that. I really would."

CHAPTER 27

The gin and tonic disappeared quickly from Charles Blumfield's glass. He glared at the woman next to him in the Winter Palace Bar. "So I get a separate room because you have the hots for some stud you just met. Sounds foolish, Joan, not like you!" His tone was callous.

Joan braced herself. It was not easy to shake off a man like Charles. He held a big chunk of her past and cutting him out of her life was stressful. She remained composed; she had said her piece. Further explanations were useless.

Charles continued in a mocking voice. "You're carrying on with a nobody from Colorado, just when the Herihor news is about to hit! You'll blow the chance of a lifetime to participate in this historic event. I figured you to have more smarts, Joan."

"The glory will suit you perfectly, Charles. I need something more solid than a few brief words of glory."

"For God's sake, the jerk probably got to your sympathy about his dead brother. It must have been lonely in this big hotel while I was gone."

"Your cruel streak is showing, Charles! What makes you

think Eric Dunn's brother is dead?"

Blumfield recovered quickly from the careless remark. "Semaine said the fellow hasn't been heard from in a month. In the heat of this desert, that sounds deadly to me."

"Seems grim to me, too, but there's no trace of kidnapping or violence. So they're not giving up hope." Joan tried to steer the conversation to another subject. "What did Semaine have to say about Herihor?"

"I'm meeting with the professor tomorrow morning. He's about to let the local chumps squeeze us out of the whole damn deal. Good thing I'm here to put things straight."

"Semaine is not a fool, Charles. Egyptians have the upper hand here. You should know; they managed to cancel your visa a few years ago."

Blumfield's eyes narrowed. "Money talks, dear. Looks like I'm back, right?"

Her former lover's boasting sounded hollow to Joan. Suddenly the arrogant golden boy appeared to her like a brassy buffoon. The unclouded view of the man she had spent years with appeared like a stranger across the table...and a scary one at that. Something about his conversation gnawed at her—those words "his dead brother." Joan shuddered. She longed for Eric's simple decency to shield her and erase the past.

Blumfield signaled the bartender for another set up, ignoring Joan's resistance. Smiling confidently, he felt certain the girl would come to her senses. She had been lonely; now all she needed was reassurance and security and he had plenty of both. His ego, not his heart, craved the possession of this woman. Lust for power had left Charles little room for true affection; nevertheless, he yearned for the devotion of others. Joan's fidelity was crucial to Charles for other motives also. She knew too much about his comings and goings. Her absurd association with Bradford Dunn's brother was bothersome to him.

The next morning, Blumfield eyed Surry suspiciously at breakfast. "By God, this is going to make the history books, Professor."

"We may get some press in the States, but I doubt if our names appear in anything coming out of the Middle East, unless it's the obituaries," Surry stated flatly. He had been unable to shake the gloomy cloud since loading Roxy's casket on the plane. Images of Bradford, Roxy and Herihor were cluttered with images of his own demise.

"Brighten up, old man...we're on the brink of fame. The Antiquities Council won't ignore my bankroll and we are tied to the paycheck. This project will need big bucks to prepare Herihor's tomb for any kind of public opening. Stick with me; you have yourself a smoking deal. My map, my money and you get in on the recognition...not bad."

Surry Semaine's eyes glazed over. Blumfield had managed to make his lifetime ambition sound cheap and gaudy. Surry's boyhood fantasy was hopelessly entwined with a scoundrel who talked about his aspirations in terms of cash and glory. The professor yearned for the waning exuberance of his youthful sparkle as the pharaoh's gold seemed to lose its luster.

"I'm not so sure money will do the trick on this one, Charles. The Egyptian authorities have been waiting for a coup like this to jolt tourism and the economy. They want Herihor all to themselves and we're an unwelcome burden...just watch." Surry could sense his lofty ideals being dragged down by practical realities.

Blumfield found Surry's pessimism irritating. Such a bore these academic types. Nevertheless, the Arizona archaeologist's credentials were still a crucial part of the picture. "Wise up, Semaine. The bottom line is money. Watch me drop a hundred-thousand-dollar check on the Chief's desk and see how fast I get an invitation into that tomb," gloated Blumfield, remembering with satisfaction his nocturnal visit to Herihor's chamber weeks ago.

Blumfield's tirade added to the weariness that weighed on Surry's mood. "No doubt that will work," he said glumly. "It's about finances, isn't it?"

"Come to the party, Prof. Money moves mountains, not that pick and shovel you rely on."

CHAPTER 28

The men gathered in Chief Bassit's stuffy office greeted each other with forced friendliness. Blumfield's haughty swagger signaled dollars to the Egyptians, who labored to conceal loathing for the braggart. The Chief listened without expression as the smug California millionaire described his willingness to pay for a piece of the glory. Did the foolhardy Americans realize that their lives meant little to Bassit? Blumfield's access to the mighty dollar made his presence tolerable.

Bassit leaned on the arm of his chair while he absently listened to the outsider's comments, all the while wishing the two Americans would be swallowed up by the Sahara sand without a trace. He did not want to contemplate what more dead Americans would do to the already delicate diplomatic relations.

"Yes, Monsieur Blumfield, we are aware that your map helped locate the tomb. We also suspect that you received the map from an Egyptian. We know these things. You have obligated us to include you. You must not forget you are in our country, not yours."

The distrust emitted from the five sunbaked officials permeated the room. Even Blumfield, accustomed to offensive behavior, felt edgy in the sober atmosphere. The familiar smiles of the white-toothed Egyptians were nowhere in sight.

Surry had cautioned Blumfield to allow the Arabs to dominant the discussion, but the pompous fellow could not refrain from exhibiting his self-importance. Semaine stared at the maps on the wall as he spoke, trying to avoid the sight of his fellow American.

"We are honored to work with you on this great discovery. The world will soon be more aware of Egypt's glories, but we must be sure to safeguard the priceless treasures. The headlines may attract unscrupulous people."

"True," agreed Zahmid, the National Director of Museums. "Egypt's riches have been stolen many times in the past by foreigners."

"Mr. Blumfield's generosity will help make Herihor's tomb more secure when thousands of visitors come to see it," continued Surry calmly. "We recognize that the Antiquities Council has a working budget, but American contributions will be useful also."

An agreement was proposed that ten million American dollars could be raised in two years, backed with a guarantee from the Blumfield Foundation. Donations would be channeled to Egypt for museum exhibits in the United States, plus royalties from media publications and museum gift shops. The Egyptian Minister of Culture would issue the first formal press release acknowledging American archaeological participation and financial contributions. Notes from the meetings were drafted and sent to lawyers for legal forms of the commitments to be drawn up and signed.

"I would pay a good price to purchase certain Herihor artifacts for the San Francisco Art Museum," Charles whispered to the National Director during the ritual hand-shaking. He had often envisioned a museum gallery named in his honor and had already hinted to museum officials that he intended to contribute his distinguished Egyptian collection to a Blumfield Gallery. An artifact from the newly discovered Herihor tomb would add prestige to his planned legacy.

Director Zahmid stared coldly at Charles. "All of Herihor's treasures belong in Egypt. That will be certain." His statement had the sharp edge of finality.

Wanting more of everything was a habit with Charles; for him satisfaction was short-lived. He was ready to press further when Surry again soothed the growing tension among their hosts. "In the future perhaps The Blumfield Foundation can sponsor a loan of selected Herihor artifacts for an exhibit at the San Francisco Museum."

"Ha! The entire world will want to see these treasures, not just Americans," remarked Zahmid abruptly. "That is another discussion. We have immediate things to take care of."

Important action included the transfer of 100,000 dollars from Blumfield's stateside bank to the coffers of the Antiquities Council, plus securing a certified promissory note for additional monies. With that accomplished and the submission of a donation schedule from the American Research Center in Cairo, the Egyptians agreed to acknowledge the American team in an international press release.

The public announcement was scheduled for November 4, the anniversary of the 1922 discovery of Tutankhamen's tomb. Before the official press release, details of Herihor's tomb remained guarded while administrators inventoried, documented and transferred the most fragile treasures to the Cairo Museum. The huge rose quartz sarcophagus would remain in situ for admirers to view when safety measures for visitors were approved.

A skilled crew of trusted workmen was engaged to install electric lighting, handrails, and other safety features which included low barriers around prized artifacts. The workers were given a bonus to remain closed-mouthed about their participation. Rumors persisted that a valuable stash had been found in the West Valley but facts continued to be vague.

CHAPTER 29

Preventing Blumfield from leaking his splendid accomplishments to the American media was a struggle. Unaccustomed to restraints, Charles yearned to break the news of the discovery and be first in line for recognition. Surry pleaded with him as Fatime's Mercedes drove toward the West Valley to meet with Chief Bassit.

"Wise up, man!" Surry tried to curb the contempt in his voice. "You ignored the local rules before and got kicked out of the country. Egyptians call the shots here and they're capable of ejecting us any time they want. In fact, we could end up like Roxy and Bradford! Use some tact while we're on the discovery site...for everyone's sake."

"Cut the drama, Semaine," injected Charles as he watched Fatime slow down at the checkpoint barrier. "Your pal, Bradford Dunn, is probably holed up with some native beauty sunbathing by the Nile." The comment silenced Surry. He turned his head and glared out the window at the barren hills.

Fatime was recognized at the guardhouse. Generous tips in the past had been appreciated and the vehicle was greeted with stoic recognition. The barricade lifted as the car continued toward the main road leading to the Valley of the Kings until it reached the narrow turn-off to the right where a new signboard had been erected: WEST VALLEY CLOSED FOR CONSTRUCTION—NO PUBLIC ENTRY. A guard scrutinized the permit that Fatime handed him and waved them onward.

"Hopes for Bradford are not bright," Surry finally replied angrily. "If he were kidnapped, ransom would have been demanded by now. Personally, I doubt he's still alive." It was the first time Surry verbalized his worst fears to himself or anyone else.

"Perhaps Herihor is sending us a message about disturbing his tomb." Blumfield's flip remark caused Fatime's steely eyes to glance in the rear view mirror.

"I'm not one to believe in curses, but we've had rotten luck since stumbling into that crypt." Surry's voice drifted off into a melancholy trance. Valerie was scheduled back in Egypt soon. He missed her.

Security around the entrance of Amenhotep's tomb had intensified. Burly soldiers from the National Army were positioned on the surrounding cliffs, their professionalism noticeably more rigid than the lethargic watchmen assigned to the usual tourist areas. With a keen eye, one could spot far off rifle barrels glistening in the hot sun. Blumfield's composure was shaken as he stepped from the car into the militant surroundings. It was evident that his checkbook did not govern here.

Bassit's assistant greeted the Americans as they climbed the slope toward Amenhotep's tomb. Surry's original tunnel from the first pillared hall had been enlarged and was still being used by archaeologists and workers, while a crew continued to work feverishly to clear the nearby main entrance to Herihor's tomb before the official press conference.

"Getting in is a lot easier now that the tunnel is wider," commented Surry as Charles struggled behind him in the crude passageway.

Remembering his clandestine visit, Blumfield's self-satisfied smirk went unnoticed in the shadows. "Yeah, I can imagine what it was like on hands and knees."

Each time Surry entered Herihor's hallowed chamber his earthly cares left him. He felt lighter, suspended in a moment of elation. Beside him Blumfield stood transfixed, his superior attitude dissolved in veneration. Temporary flood lights made the gold leaf stars on the domed ceiling shine brilliantly. A current of excitement flowed from the whispers among the scholars taking inventory of king's burial treasures.

Sitting on the floor among priceless artifacts was the chief curator from the Cairo Museum. Two white-gloved assistants worked nearby at folding tables loaded with video cameras, surgical tools and preservation material. Herihor's sanctified resting place had taken on the air of a scientific laboratory. After centuries of nonchalance, Egyptian specialists had become experts about preserving their illustrious history.

Along one wall were richly-decorated cedar chests containing fine bed linens, table coverings and woven cotton clothing. Several low chairs, graceful wooden tables, baskets of games and other small items were stacked in one corner waiting to be transported to Cairo. A life-size torso, complete with the crowned head, stared out from a niche in the wall. Noting the number of tiny pin punctures in the figure's porous wood, the curator explained it had been used as a mannequin to custom-fit the pharaoh's wardrobe.

A princely chariot made of inlaid bentwood lay against another wall. Gold-plated gods and goddesses in various sizes watched over the royal furnishings, casting eerie reflections as the workmen's lights bounced off the profusion of decorative gold leaf. The magical scene filled even the impervious American millionaire with awe and managed to lift Surry from the doldrums.

The Egyptian team accepted Surry and Charles with courtesy, but their welcome lacked the cordial friendliness that existed among their fellow countrymen. The Americans had been asked to leave their cameras behind and the two men were not included in the video documentation. Determined to preserve what was left of the professional relationship, Surry adhered to Bassit's orders and reluctantly agreed to the imposed limitations. He did not want his career goals to end in a puff of banishment. Surry pulled out his Apple notebook while Charles perused the piles of ancient riches.

Bassit, proudly looking very much in charge, sauntered down the steps of the antechamber motioning toward the ladder placed beside the majestic sarcophagus. "Climb up and look before we remove the inner lid. It's sensational!" he stated.

The damaged outer stone cover had been removed by a pulley and rig and lay on a rubber cushion next to the massive quartz coffin. Spotlights surrounded the sarcophagus. From the top of the ladder Surry's eyes glowed as he viewed the chiseled image of the Pharaoh which was sculpted on the lid of the second gray alabaster container. The carved stone form lay with arms crossed holding a royal crook and flail, its bearded stone face staring up at the professor.

When each person had his turn at viewing the inner

coffin, pulleys were readied to lift the heavy stone covering and to proceed with the unveiling of the actual mummy. Anticipation ran high. It was evident the Curator from Cairo was in control of the examination schedule and remained unwavering in the method of revealing the mummy, as well as who would be privileged to witness the event.

Charles bristled with noticeable impatience. The whole reverent process was going too slowly for him. "Don't make trouble, Blumfield, it wouldn't take much to shut us out of all this," murmured Surry, noting the man's restlessness.

Charles scoffed. "They'll put up with us as long as they smell money." His mind flashed to the recent secretive visit to the burial chamber with Joan. The gold-trimmed rosewood statue and the photographs of the deserted crypt were testimony enough of his own ingenious resourcefulness. There would be other opportunities to outwit these peasants. He could wait.

The hushed atmosphere of the dead sovereign's sanctuary affected each person present differently, but all experienced the allusion of timelessness. The finality of death is usually more daunting to people who question reincarnation, allowing Muslims, who believe in an afterlife to appear more comfortable with mortality than most Westerners. Nevertheless, there is a cautious reverence in almost every society about disturbing the dead.

Blumfield's eyes remained transfixed on the formidable stone coffin of the once powerful ruler. The almighty kings of Egypt had considered themselves gods and saviors, yet they all ended up like this—wrapped in linen and sealed in rock. Charles felt a moment of fleeting vulnerability while standing under the cobalt blue ceiling sprinkled with gold stars.

The statuesque gods of the underworld depicted on the

walls were gradually sucking energy from Blumfield's self-imposed importance. Showing weakness of any kind made Charles uncomfortable. The poignant reminder of the inevitable end of life on earth enveloped him in an unnerving cold sweat. He had a sudden urge to escape the dark underground cavern.

"I have to go. I have an appointment in town," Charles announced to the surprised professor. "Fatime will take me. Catch a ride with Bassit."

"Sure, Charles, no problem." Surry was startled, but glad to see him go for whatever reason.

An assistant escorted Blumfield to the entrance where x-ray monitors discouraged anyone from taking souvenirs. Charles was in no mood to steal objects from a place that was capable of stealing his own strength.

He shuddered when the wave of desert heat hit his clammy skin. *Merely a case of claustrophobia*, Charles told himself in an attempt to dispel the unfamiliar panic that had gripped him. He rushed unsteadily toward Fatime's car, desperately trying to shake off the thought of one's unavoidable destiny.

"Take me to the Hilton. A good bar there. I need a drink," ordered Blumfield, grateful to feel back in command. He rode silently while passing ruins of Ramses' massive funerary temple and saw in the distance the Colossi of Memnon. The giant pair of seated seventy-foot stone statues of Amenhotep had stood on each side of the entrance to his funerary temple before it was destroyed by centuries of earthquakes, floods and thieves. The enormous figures of Amenhotep III had remained stubbornly perched on their thrones for more than three thousand years.

Monumental tributes impressed Charles. Who would revere his own memory? He deserved to be recognized in history books as the rightful discoverer of Herihor's tomb. It was his map that had led to the King's tomb. If only he could eliminate Semaine's name as he had erased Bradford Dunn's. Perhaps it could be arranged that the curse of Herihor would take care of Surry Semaine also. Many of Howard Carter's team who worked with him to find King Tut's tomb had met with misfortune. The public still feasted on the mysterious curse of the 1922 discovery. Blumfield's mood brightened. He had the cunning and cash to make things happen.

Fatime's black Mercedes sped across the sleek Nasser Bridge, slowing down for the road patrol to wave him through. The Arab driver and his passenger ate lunch at the Hilton's terrace café which overlooked drifting *feluccas* in the easy flow of the Nile. An afternoon of chilled martinis carried Charles further into a spell of devious schemes. When he returned to the Winter Palace that afternoon, he was not concerned with Joan Kaufman or anyone else. He went straight to his suite thinking only of the illustrious Charles Blumfield and the glory that would soon surround him.

CHAPTER 30

Eric Dunn insisted that he and Joan change hotels, distancing themselves from Blumfield and the Winter Palace. They settled into the Mercure Hotel a mile down the riverbank, where they could begin a new day in fresh surroundings.

Hopes for finding Bradford alive slowly diminished. One less human on earth meant little in a country struggling with a history of impoverished masses. Officials at the American Embassy were obligated to pursue the case, but they, too, became disheartened. Manhunts in the sprawling Sahara Desert were perilous and discouraging when temperatures soared above 130 degrees Fahrenheit.

The desert terrain was constantly changing while daily winds shifted enormous mounds of sand from place to place, making it doubtful that even Kom could have found where he buried Bradford's body. In six months, a human would be baked to a leathery carcass. The only traces Eric had of his brother were the belongings left behind in the hotel room on that morning of the fateful taxi ride to the bull pits.

Eric conscientiously folded Brad's clothing and placed the items in his brother's aluminum suitcase, then went to the Nefertari's reception desk to settle charges for the surveyor's room. The simple items that were left behind were meager offerings for a mother who waited in Colorado for her eldest son. Eric could not keep the news from her any longer, knowing there would soon be leaks in Colorado newspapers.

Eric proceeded with the depressing duties of leaving Luxor without his brother or any hope of seeing him again. Both he and Joan shared the impulse to get far away from the distressing events that plagued their stay in Egypt. It seemed the right time to test their feelings on home territory, hoping the bond between them would survive the more unadventurous scene in America.

The graveyard of the sacred bulls beckoned Eric for one final pilgrimage to a place where Bradford was last heard of alive. Joan felt compelled to close a chapter and bid goodbye to Charles Blumfield. She suggested a meeting at the Winter Palace Royal Bar.

"So you're really taken with this guy," mocked Charles. "Leaving the expedition now is a big price to pay for a new boyfriend."

"You can call it what you like. To me, it's more than that…time will tell. You're a married man, Charles; there wasn't much of a chance for you and me."

"Our minds soared together, my dear. That's better than a marriage contract."

"You always have an answer, but on your own terms. I'm ready for the stability of a real partnership. Enough looking back, let's try to make this a pleasant goodbye. What's the word on Herihor?"

"Well, you're about to miss out on the sensation of the

century. This thing is richer than we thought. It's going to be a media blockbuster and you would have been one of the insiders, Joan."

"A lot of good that did Eric's brother or Roxy Morgan. They're not here to enjoy the sensational news either…sounds like a pharaoh's curse at work."

"Curse, hell," scoffed Charles. "Those two were careless, trying to play heroes in a foreign country. One can't be reckless in this part of the world."

"Do you think Bradford Dunn is gone forever?"

"Didn't know the fellow, Joan, and probably never will. It's not likely a man lost in the Sahara for months will show up healthy. He's probably parched somewhere in the sand by now."

The blunt remark made Joan flinch. Her former lover's coldness became painfully clear as she viewed him through eyes void of sentiment. "You're cruel, Charles. You make a man's life sound meaningless."

"Some lives are just plain insignificant and you know it. Achievers have to make important thing happen. That's reality."

"There are people who do good deeds quietly without thoughts of rewards and Bradford Dunn seemed to be that kind of man. Did Fatime ever mention talk in the village about Dunn?"

With a glance of annoyance, Charles straightened up in his chair. "I've never asked, Joan. I have zero interest in your new friend or his brother. I have better things to do."

"We all have reasons to move on, Charles. My work for you is done; you can keep tabs on Professor Semaine yourself. I'm ready to go back to the States, but I wanted to say goodbye in person. I'll watch for your name in the headlines."

"I can't picture you and that guy living in a log cabin in Colorado, Joanie. Good luck." Charles motioned for the check. He gave her a cool pat on the back, thinking it was just as well that the girl was on her way. Her questions about Brad Dunn were bothersome.

Numbness gripped Joan as she drifted out of the elegant hotel and down the steps to the flower-lined sidewalk. Seeing clearly the contemptible nature of a former lover had been a blow to her self-esteem, realizing she had been under his spell for too long. How could she have so willingly taken part in his depraved schemes? It was surprising to her that devotion could evaporate so quickly. It was an unsettling awareness to wake up and find a new person occupying one's own skin.

Joan breathed deeply and pulled herself erect as she walked to the line of horse-drawn carriages waiting in the sun. "The Mercure Hotel," she stated boldly, handing the driver a ten-pound note. The determined tone of her voice discouraged any bickering about the fare.

Charles shrugged off Joan's departure with indifference. There was nothing of importance she could divulge about his recent actions. She was a good lay but had no imagination, no ambition. Actually having her out of the way lightened his mind. The intrigue and mysteries of the Sahara were enough for him. After centuries of countless rulers in Egypt, he knew that laws of this desert country had gone through many changes and continued to be flexible. Charles was comfortable doing business where money could cut through bureaucracy and he was able to buy anything he wanted. This place suited the way Charles Blumfield liked to operate.

After cooling off in the shower, Charles admired his distinguished image in the mirror. He smiled confidently as he pushed back his wet hair with a monogrammed silver brush. He cautioned himself not to appear too affluent for the meeting with a mere minor officer who had noticed him at the tomb and now wanted to meet him with "articles of interest to sell."

CHAPTER 31

After American donation commitments for the Herihor project were officially filed with the Department of Culture, the National Director of Museums and Chief Bassit proceeded with necessary arrangements for an International Press Conference. Optimism pulsated through Egypt's State Department. Surely the news of this superb discovery would revive the sagging tourist industry which had been interrupted by terrorist turmoil.

The first money that Blumfield donated was immediately used to construct a more serviceable asphalt road leading to the site of Herihor's tomb. Confident that their investments would bring generous returns, government agencies had provided additional funds for restoration of the tomb entrance, safety facilities, and tourism amenities. Elaborate programs for a year-long celebration were scheduled while the complex infrastructure of passageways for the expected influx of media teams and tourists moved forward.

Minister Zahmid studied the files of the famous 1922 Tutankhamen events. Egyptian authorities were determined that Americans would not dominate the Herihor publicity as the British had when Lord Carnarvon and Howard Carter captured the imagination of the world for the entire decade, giving little credit to the citizens of Egypt.

Rumors of a ghostly curse still hovered around the Tut legend. Zahmid did little to dispel talk concerning a Herihor curse; in fact, he quietly approved of the sinister gossip, which was certain to arouse attention in press releases designed for the general public. The mysterious deaths of the two Americans connected with the discovery team were of little consequence to public relations representatives except to further promote mysterious desert intrigue. In Director Bassit's opinion, the mummy's curse had not done quite enough. With the donation contracts form the Blumfield Foundation securely committed and recorded, Blumfield himself had become an unnecessary nuisance.

Hundreds of adventurers had disappeared in the Sahara Desert throughout the ages and Bassit felt that most of them were probably far more commendable than the loathsome Monsieur Blumfield. Bassit recognized that Charles Blumfield was a risk taker and unfortunately risks often lead to tragic events. When gamblers meet up with bad luck, ruinous results can take place.

Aziz Habid was one of Bassit's trusted young officers. They had both come from the same village of Medinet Habu and Bassit had dutifully helped the teenager obtain a recommendation for military school. Aziz never forgot the favor, remaining fiercely loyal to Bassit since his graduation as an officer in the Egyptian army.

Lieutenant Habid enjoyed a comfortable lifestyle in Luxor. He owned a three-room brick house on the canal, drove a car supplied by the army and earned enough to support a wife, four children and various other members of his family. Although he was not exceptionally brilliant, he was clever enough to be helpful to those who controlled his promotions. Aziz was flattered to be chosen by Bassit to carry out such a troublesome and confidential assignment. He was instructed to assume the role of a corrupt guard who had artifacts to sell to an American collector named Charles Blumfield.

The group of loyal henchmen surrounding Chief Bassit wove a web of intrigue which took care of miscellaneous duties not covered by conventional means. Government laws and judicial courts functioned in Luxor only when matters could not be handled by local traditional methods. Europeans and Americans visiting Egypt were often considered naïve in their complicated ways of getting things done and their Western habits were tolerated primarily for reasons of economic diplomacy.

Charles Blumfield was an obnoxious example of Western attitudes of superiority and was regarded by several local officials to be unsuitable to share in a world-class event that would be forever inscribed in Egyptian archives. The earnest Professor Semaine might be acceptable as an academic associate, but the boastful millionaire from San Francisco had misjudged his usefulness. Bassit was aware that he was not the only one to harbor hostility for greedy foreigners who had stolen Egypt's treasures and he considered it a duty to avenge past transgressions against his country whenever the opportunity arose.

Cunning schemes to eliminate irritating obstacles are common in third-world countries. Unknowing tourists visit developing countries in a fog of false safety, relying on their own country's democratic privileges which often do not apply in exotic cultures.

Blumfield possessed a skeptical and wary attitude, but his confidence was enhanced and his prudence sometimes diminished by the ability to buy his way out of trouble when necessary. Up until now, his brashness had served him well, but there is a subtle point when courage can disintegrate into recklessness. Charles miscalculated the line drawn when his checkbook became useless against old world pride and tactics.

Charles was enjoying particularly high spirits as he swayed gently in the back of a black leather carriage drawn by trotting horses. The languid night air caressed his face as the wooden-spoke wheels hummed along the blacktop road bordering the Nile.

Robed villagers clustered on benches along the river socializing in the cool evening air. For the first time since his arrival in Luxor, Charles allowed the local atmosphere of eternity to imbue him with tranquility while he gazed at the slender palm trees swaying above the open buggy. The voice on the phone had instructed him to come alone and he was pleased that he had followed that suggestion and could enjoy the restful moment by himself. The thought of viewing precious artifacts offered by a lowly laborer intrigued him.

The articles had been vaguely described to him as items from Herihor's tomb which had somehow been separated from the cargo being transported to the Cairo Museum. The story was credible enough after hearing of Fatime's reports about the secretive, but steady, transfer of Herihor's burial goods to Cairo for examination. Local rumors were at times remarkably accurate and well worth the dollars and cigarettes Blumfield offered natives for gossip on the street.

Blumfield paid regularly to be informed about the continuing restoration activities going on in Herihor's tomb. He was aware that many crates of treasures were being shipped downstream to Cairo and he was also informed which objects stayed in the tomb. Charles was enthralled with reports about the extraordinary objects found in the tomb but had little interest in the drudgery of the sweaty labor involved. The assurance that he would be respected as a member of the discovery team when the press conference took place was satisfaction enough.

A man with Blumfield's appetite for esteem and rewards can rarely be satisfied and the curious phone call from a guard offering "important items" for sale was irresistible to his insatiable desire for more of everything. The small rosewood statue of Herihor, the jasper carving of Anubis and the gold toe stalls in his possession were mere teasers for more precious possessions.

Since ancient times, archaeologists, workers and even public officials were known to carry off a few small tomb relics for their own gain. Artifacts could easily disappear from the scores of wooden boxes as workmen nailed the lids down in preparation for transfer. A small stolen statue or carved game set could provide an undercover deal that would keep a laborer's family nourished for months.

Charles took great pleasure in his airy carriage ride while envisioning himself as a resourceful adventurer on the trail of yet another conquest. All was going well: his skillful re-entry into Egypt, the impending world recognition he would share for Herihor's discovery and even the timely unloading of Joan Kaufman before she claimed a stake in the honors. There would be no shortage of female admirers once fame was added to his many attributes.

He spotted the lone man draped in a gray robe loitering near the English cemetery. The dirt path beside the canal which bordered the cemetery was the designated meeting place. "Stop at the canal," ordered Charles, leaning to the side of the carriage as it approached the turbaned figure in the shadows of the oleanders. "Do you have something for sale?" he inquired in a hushed voice.

"Yes, something of interest. Follow me. The carriage cannot enter here, let it go. I shall drive you to your hotel."

Overcoming a moment of hesitation, Charles stepped down from the unsteady buggy. One had to be cautious with black market rogues. He pulled a twenty-pound note from his roll of Egyptian money and handed it to the driver, patting another money belt under his shirt. He was prepared to deal in dollars or Egyptian pounds if an offer was to his liking.

"What do you have?" inquired Charles bluntly, peering down the unlit alleyway along the cemetery wall. It reminded him of a classic biblical scene as he viewed the maze of mud-brick structures clinging to each other under the palms bordering the murky canal. Little squares of faint light escaped from the few small openings in the thick walls.

"You will see my brother's house very soon. You will be happy," muttered the native.

Dodging donkey dung in the shadowy light, Blumfield's nerves were tense in the unfamiliar old world surroundings. He would have felt more secure if Fatime were there to explain each strange sound and smell that fluttered from this humble hive of humanity.

As the two men walked further from the main road, Charles grew anxious as he slipped in slimy grass near the canal bank. What had seemed like an exciting quest for art objects only an hour before was now being diminished by shadowy scenery. Glancing over his shoulder at the dull glimmer of lights from town, he felt the urge to turn back, when, unexpectedly, a dark figure pushed open a bamboo gate, motioning the two men to enter.

Beaded lamps barely illuminated the stark room. A

framed poster of the nation's president smiled down from the honored position above an armless couch. A carved wooden chest topped with a television and a low wicker table were the only other furnishings, except for several colorful floor cushions scattered on the floor.

"This is my brother, Mohammed." Aziz nodded to the bearded man who welcomed them. "He will bring us tea and I will show the pieces. Please sit."

The place suited the small-time thieves, mused Charles. It was the first time he had been in a native worker's home and he noted the meager details for the dramatic story he would tell his friends in San Francisco. The ambiance of the sparse room was a world away from the comforts of the Winter Palace Hotel.

Feeling more confident, Charles sat on the lumpy couch and prepared to endure the traditional courtesy of mint tea before doing business. Aziz crouched crossed-legged on a cushion near the table facing his guest.

"If you become owner of certain objects, you must tell that you discovered them yourself. You cannot come back to me. I will deny all. Such relics are now forbidden to leave our country. Do you agree to this?" Aziz stated sternly.

"That is not a problem for me," Charles responded, eager to spend as little time as possible in the strange household.

When the brass tray with glasses of hot tea was placed on the table, Mohammed left the room and returned with a bulky leather bag, which he gently lowered on the table. The tan-skinned men displayed toothy smiles, obviously proud of their booty. The sack sat undisturbed as Aziz handed his guest the syrupy tea. The thick, sweet mixture, made from local mint leaves, and the offered cigarettes were considered generous gestures of hospitality from humble people who had little to give. Similar tea customs had greeted Charles in numerous Arab shops that he traded in, but the ritual bored him and he wanted to get on with business. Sipping the mint-flavored liquid, Charles winced at its unusual bitterness, suspecting his hosts had skimped on sugar.

"Let's see what you have," insisted the visitor, losing patience with the scruffy characters.

"Yes, you will see." Aziz reached gingerly into the sack and withdrew a narrow object carelessly wrapped in a thin scarf. Spreading the flimsy fabric on the table, he removed a twelve-inch golden dagger in a sheaf elaborately inlayed with semi-precious stones. Removing the knife from its case, he handed it to Charles.

The dagger fit perfectly in his grip and was heavier than he expected. Charles wrapped his fingers around the thickly-encrusted handle, suddenly feeling empowered with a sensation of nobility. Blumfield's eyes glimmered as he scrutinized the exquisite workmanship of the etched blade. A finely-wrought cartouche was evident in the center of the golden knife's sheaf.

Attempting to appear unmoved, Charles motioned toward the sack for another item. His pulse jumped again at the sight of a small female statue wearing gold bracelets and a jewel-encrusted collar. Her diaphanous bronze gown flowed over rounded breasts with narrow bands of ivory trim at the waist and hem. The pounding in Blumfield's chest seemed almost audible. *I can't be so hard up to start palpitating over a goddess*, he wondered as he felt a slight dizziness.

Staring through dark, narrow eyes, Aziz laid two more funerary objects on the table—a thick metal offering plate edged in gems and a rosewood case containing a rock crystal checkerboard.

The museum-quality items lying on the simple table glowed as if they carried light from another world. The artifacts looked even more stunning when seen in the room's austere decor. Blumfield's eyes glistened as he caressed each prized piece. "What is your price," he asked in a strange voice, as he struggled to remain calm. His insides were pounding and he felt unsteady, even feverish.

"These things are special. You have the first chance. I must have three thousand American dollars," answered Aziz slowly, noticing the perspiration forming on Blumfield's brow. The charade was over. Captain Aziz knew there was no need to negotiate further. There would be no exchange of objects or money. The lethal brew of oleander tea was serving its purpose.

It was not easy to pierce the inflated self-worth of Charles Blumfield, but illness in a strange land was a fate he feared. The surging palpitations in his chest could no longer be ignored and now he recognized they were not merely tremors of excitement over the golden goods. The dingy little room became dimmer and swirled around him. Mushy sweat soaked his expensive shirt and he became too weak to protest when his host caught him as his body lurched toward the hard earthen floor.

"Not me...not me," he murmured deliriously. "Not by common thieves..."

Aziz and his brother left enough money in Blumfield's pocket to dismiss suspicion of robbery. By cover of night the men transported the lifeless American in a military vehicle through narrow alleyways to the back wall of the Winter Palace gardens. Chief Bassit had provided a key to the gardener's gate through which Charles Blumfield was delivered at three in the morning to a lounge chair among the hotel's thick grove of trees.

Mr. Blumfield, the guest occupying Suite 250, was found at daybreak near the bird sanctuary slumped in a chair, an obvious heart attack victim. Further rumors circulated about Herihor's curse.

CHAPTER 32

It was a glorious day for the Minister of Culture and Chief Bassit. Members of the international press had responded enthusiastically to the scheduled announcement of the sensational discovery of the lost Egyptian king. The three hundred seats and fifty camera spaces in the grand ballroom of the Winter Palace Hotel were immediately spoken for by eager television and publication executives from around the globe. Royal mummies, ancient treasures and tomb curses were choice feasts for the voracious appetite of world media correspondents.

Elaborate press kits issued by the Department of Culture focused on Egypt's illustrious history, the fifteenth century B.C. royal dynasty and the recent discovery of a lost tomb containing the riches of King Herihor. There was mention of Professor Surry Semaine and his American research team and Arizona State University was cited as a supporting institution. The Blumfield Foundation appeared near the top of the list of financial benefactors.

The tall elegant windows of the ballroom which welcomed dignitaries and members of the press overlooked the hotel's lush gardens and attractive aviary cages. The shady magnolia trees, rambling brick walkways, blooming hibiscus and huge swimming pool gave no hint of the country's underprivileged population. Foreign tourists were generally unaware that the cleaning staff of this opulent hotel was considered among the fortunate wage earners. The golden glories of the ancient pharaohs did little to shed light on the lives of their disadvantaged descendants in the twenty-first century. Pride of a magnificent heritage was about all that remained of the sophisticated legacy left from the days of the dazzling Egyptian Kingdom. With masses of their tangible treasures carried off in the past by foreign adventurers, contemporary Egyptian authorities made it clear that Herihor's treasures would belong entirely to the land where the king had ruled.

Seated at a long mahogany table facing masses of microphones, video cameras and an audience of journalists were Egypt's Minister of Culture, the Chief of the Supreme Council of Antiquities, the Director of Museums, Chief Inspector Bassit and Egypt's Press Secretary.

Professor Semaine and Valerie Semaine were seated with other distinguished guests in the front row of the audience, clearly not in a position to answer questions from the press. Beside them sat American Ambassador Malone and his press attaché. A rather tardy invitation had been sent to Charles Blumfield's widow, who declined due to the rigors of settling Blumfield's probate issues in California.

The six glass showcases containing choice pieces from the Pharaoh's funerary stockpile were guarded by unsmiling uniformed soldiers. It was one of the few opportunities in recent years for the media to report on the splendor of Egypt rather than the images of terrorism and conflict. The crowd's enthusiasm was nourished by plentiful supplies of

Omar Khayyam wine and local delicacies offered by waiters in pasha pants and scarlet jackets.

Surry and Valerie exchanged sideward glances while Director Zahmid proudly pointed out the boundaries of Herihor's tomb on the enormous map in the corner of the room. Ambassador Malone had fully agreed with Professor Semaine's decision to cooperate respectfully with the announcement program planned by Egyptian authorities. After all, it was their country, their ancestors and, in reality, the tomb was fully in their control. If Surry and his colleagues had hopes of future participation in the Herihor venture, it appeared imperative to remain on friendly terms with the controlling powers.

Had he lived, Charles Blumfield would have undoubtedly bullied his way into the spotlight and again he would have found out that, in modern Egypt, it is the Egyptians who have the upper hand when it comes to their heritage. Charles was no longer present to make demands even though his financial commitment to Herihor's rebirth was gratefully accepted and acknowledged.

Director Zahmid graciously introduced the American ambassador and Professor Semaine after the formal announcement had been made. When the American contingent was credited, cameras flashed and American reporters jumped on the opportunity to incorporate a North American connection to the world-class treasure trove. After the public figure at the head table answered the round of questions, the official conference was adjourned. Middle Eastern and Asian journalists continued to snap photos of Chief Bassit and his team with little attention directed toward Professor Semaine; however, television and press correspondents from North America went directly to the Professor and his wife for comments on their role in the discovery.

Media executives clamored for the right to visit the celebrated burial chamber. The glossy photos of the tomb enclosed in press kits merely increased their curiosity. Through a lottery selection, thirty journalists were selected for a guided tour of the tomb site. Adventure stories sold well and foreign correspondents were elated for a reprieve from covering negative news in the Middle East.

Details about "the tomb curse" was irresistible copy for many reporters in spite of Professor Semaine's objection to comment on the subject. He answered inquiries about his American associates with brief details concerning the unfortunate circumstances that had taken place during the past summer. Probing interviewers asked Surry and Valerie if they considered themselves next in line for the "pharaoh's curse."

"A career in archaeology is not for the faint-hearted," he answered, attempting to maintain his patience with the annoying questions.

Surry and Valerie were relieved to be back in the United States looking at the peaceful sunset that framed the McDowell Mountains in a purple glow. For the first few days they felt depleted in both mind and body with just enough determination to unpack and stuff dusty khakis and underwear in the washer while slowly airing out their minds from turbulent summer events. The couple stayed shielded off from the world in their own home for an entire week.

As the days, passed the ancient wonders of Egypt seemed like a far-off fantasy even though an Arizona sunrise reaching over the nearby hills was reminiscent of an early Luxor dawn. Surry was happy to be drinking familiar Starbucks coffee in his own kitchen rather than in his beloved world of past civilizations and underworld riches.

The task of sorting through the stacks of congratulatory letters, newspaper clippings and speaking requests was a bittersweet process for the newly celebrated couple. Indeed, the Semaines were pleased with the enormous interest in Herihor; however, they both found it difficult to shake off the tarnished details of the past summer that surrounded their lifelong dream of discovery. Surry suffered waves of guilt each time he came across mention of Bradford Dunn or Roxy Morgan when their names were bandied about in sleazy articles referring to the "pharaoh's curse" or the "underworld's revenge." At times, when Surry pondered his three colleagues who had met with fatal outcomes, he himself wondered if by some weird possibility it could be retaliation from the underground world.

Lecture and interview offers kept Valerie and her newly appointed assistant buried in correspondence and scheduling duties. With book offers pouring in for Professor Semaine and a flood of publicity for Arizona State University, Semaine became a new hero on campus. The Dean approved a year-long sabbatical, enabling Doctor Semaine to accept prestigious lecture engagements and enough free time to work on a book.

His request to return to Luxor for continuing documentation of Herihor's Tomb was slow in receiving approval from Egypt's Minister of Culture. Due to the financial support of the Blumfield Foundation and mounting donations available to Professor Semaine, he and Valerie were approved to return to the Herihor Project the following summer. A year away from the stressful scene was welcomed by the Semaines. It would take time to reconcile the depressing events the team had encountered in Luxor.

Valerie maintained the appearance of order in her husband's life. When Surry demanded solitude, somehow she found a quiet place for him by turning off the phone and locking the door while he was alone in his study. The rush of attention did not distort the professor's ego, which was kept in check by the gnawing awareness of the price paid for the fleeting fame. He dedicated his new book to Bradford and Roxy, with royalties transferred to the Dunn-Morgan Scholarship Fund for Ancient History Studies.

"Was it all worth it, Val?" questioned Surry quietly one evening while they sat on the terrace watching the rosy tones of evening spread across the desert landscape.

"It was a boyhood dream that became a reality, my dear. We were merely too naïve to consider what the price might be. Dreams are small but history is big; future generations will forget the dreadful cost we paid for finding Herihor."

"You're right, Val, history forgets small details. We'll carry on. There's more for us out there in that desert. Next summer will be better, won't it?!"

TOMB OF HERIHOR

ABOUT THE AUTHOR

Edith Kunz is a graduate of Colorado Women's College/University of Denver and retired from a career in retail merchandising with Goldwater's Department Store. She serves on the advisory board of the Center for Film, Media and Popular Culture at Arizona State University. A committed Francophile since childhood, she has chosen to live part of each year in Paris, France. During the winter she resides in Scottsdale, Arizona, with her husband. Their adult daughters live in the USA.

Edith, a committed Francophile since childhood, states that the contrast between the desert beauty of Arizona and the urbanity of Paris invigorates her senses. *Fatale: How French Women Do It*, Edith's book describing the mystique of French women (sexy, smart and chic), published in 2000 and available in its third printing, is still in demand—no doubt because her work reflects an in-depth observation of the French, a grasp of history and, not least, a formidable wit!

Made in the USA
Charleston, SC
02 April 2016